I HAVE A SECRET

Cheryl Bradshaw

This book is a work of fiction. Names, characters, places, businesses, and incidents either are the products of the author's imagination or are used in a fictitious manner. Any similarity to events or locales or persons, living or dead, is entirely coincidental and should be recognized as such.

First edition April 2012

Copyright © 2012 by Cheryl Bradshaw

Cover Design Copyright 2012 © Reese Dante
All rights reserved.

ISBN-13: 978-1475190816
ISBN-10: 1475190816

For updates on Cheryl and her books:

Blog: cherylbradshawbooks.blogspot.com
Web: cherylbradshaw.com
Facebook: Cheryl Bradshaw Author Page
Twitter: @cherylbradshaw

No part of this publication may be reproduced, stored or transmitted, in any form, or by any means whatsoever (electronic, mechanical, etc.) without the prior written permission and consent of the author.

ALSO BY CHERYL BRADSHAW

Black Diamond Death, (Sloane Monroe Book #1)
Murder in Mind (Sloane Monroe Book #2)
Sloane Monroe Series Boxed Set (Books 1-3)
Stranger in Town (Sloane Monroe Book #4)
Bed of Bones (Sloane Monroe Book #5)

Author praise for Black Diamond Death:

The tone reminded me of Robert B. Parker's novels, so if you're missing the likes of Spenser and Sunny Randall, I'd say that Cheryl Bradshaw looks to be a worthy successor. Highly recommended!
--Chris Stout, Author of Days of Reckoning

For an author's first book, Black Diamond Death, is one that drew me in with the prologue. I've downloaded the next one in the Sloane Monroe series, Murder in Mind, because I enjoyed the first book and I have the feeling I'm going to find an even better novel with the second one.
--S. Warfield, Vine Voice, Top 500 Reviewer

Author praise for Murder in Mind:

Only once in a while do you come upon a novel that sweeps you literally off your feet. The pot-boiling tension in this story is out of this world. Cheryl Bradshaw can write like the pros did at the Turn of the 20th Century. This is an instant classic. Absolutely sensational indisputably.
-- Glen Cantrell, Author of The Resume

Bradshaw writes a great thriller, with likeable characters, and a taunt timeline that keeps you reading way past lights-out.
-- Robin Landry, Vine Voice, Top 500 Reviewer

DEDICATION

This book is dedicated to the many friends I attended Tehachapi High School with during the years of 1989 to 1992, with special consideration to my own class—1991. I've never forgotten my roots, and this novel is a tribute to that.

***

ACKNOWLEDGEMENTS

To Stephen King for giving me permission to quote you in my novel. You had me at *Carrie*, and have kept me there throughout the years. I appreciate your willingness to extend even the simplest courtesy to me. Long live the King!

My husband Justin for always asking me how long it will be until the book is done – definitely a driving force.

To the Tehachapi Chief of Police, Jeff Kermode, for answering my homicide questions. And to John Pitko, Eric Harris, and Greg Hewgill for answering my historical questions.

Many thanks to my new editor, Janet Green, my fabulous beta readers, Becky Fagnant and Amy Jirsa-Smith, and my fantastic formatter, Dafeenah Jameel. Also, a big shout out to the best cover designer since sliced bread, Reese Dante.

To my friends and family for your continued support.

And finally to Mumford and Sons. *Timshel*, is the theme song for this book.

"It's not me who can't keep a secret. It's the people I tell that can't."
-Abraham Lincoln

CHAPTER 1

Doug Ward stood on the ship's deck and gazed across the calm waves of an evening sea. The cool ocean breeze brushed past his face and clung to it like little particles of mist, but he didn't seem to notice. The scotch in his hand was his fifth of the night, or the sixth or seventh—he couldn't remember. Most nights he drank until he passed out, and tonight would be no exception. He'd drink himself into oblivion if it meant never hearing another one of his classmates sing the karaoke version of M.C. Hammer's "U Can't Touch This."

Twenty years had passed since anyone called him "Douggie", but tonight he'd heard it shouted from every corner of the stuffy room that contained him. All he wanted was to get away from it, so he left the crowd at the costume party behind to sing their hearts out while he pondered the long list of life's regrets in solitude. Rounding out the top five was his decision to take the high school reunion cruise in the first place. But there was little he could do about that now.

Two more days, he thought, *and this trip will be all over.*

Doug's memories of high school had faded through the years until he hadn't remembered much of anything. It all seemed like the blur of someone else's life, as if the experiences he recalled weren't really his anymore. He had flashes of memories here and there, but only one solid enough to stand the test of time. And that was the one he'd tried his hardest to forget, but no amount of alcohol would ever drown it out. Not completely.

Often times Doug thought about what he'd change if he could go back in time and do it all over again. He envisioned himself at the fork in the road and often thought about what it would have been like had he chosen to go in the other direction. Maybe he wouldn't have gone through life with all the nightmares that plagued him, or the secrets that gnawed at his insides like a thief in the darkness trying to find his way out of a dense, black fog surrounding him on all sides.

"There you are," a voice said behind him.

Doug rotated his body around and faced Trista, his wife. She looked exquisite in her black satin vampire gown that hugged every curve of her petite frame. Her cocoa-colored hair fell in loose curls around her shoulders, and her lips were stained the perfect shade of red. It didn't matter how many years had come and gone since they'd married, she still remained the most beautiful woman he'd ever seen.

"I'm sorry, honey. I just needed a moment alone," he said.

"Everyone is looking for you," she said. "They want to know what happened to the life of the party."

He rattled the ice cubes in his glass around and shook his head. "You know I haven't been worthy of that title for a very long time."

She shrugged. "You can't help how people remember you, Mr. Prom King. And I thought you should know your queen is getting lonely in there without you."

Doug managed to crack a smile. He hated to disappoint her. "I need a few more minutes, okay? And then I'll come in."

Trista wrapped her arms around him, stared into his eyes and whispered, "I'll be waiting," and then she brushed her lips across his and turned and went back inside.

Doug winced when she touched him. Not because her affections were unwanted, but because he knew how much he'd let her down over the years. He hadn't lived up to the man he should have been—not as a husband, a father, any of it. And yet she stayed while he wasted away. He knew he didn't deserve her, and that made him feel even worse.

So many times Doug tried to pick himself up again, for his wife and their kids. But no matter how many twelve-step programs he went to, it always ended the same way, with one eyeball staring down the bottom of a bottle until he'd finished every last drop. Most nights he woke up in his bed not knowing how he got there, and he'd turn and gaze upon Trista who was snuggled up next to him. In those moments of serenity he vowed the next day would be different. But when the sun rose and brought a chance to start anew, he was too weak and couldn't get out the door without at least one drink.

Doug turned back and stared out to the sea again, but the night had bathed the sea in black, and he couldn't see much of anything anymore besides the mirrored glow of the moon across still waters. He sighed; it was time to go back inside.

Beside the door a shadow emerged and gravitated in his direction. Doug hunched over to get a better look, but his eyes played tricks on him, and everything was a haze. "I'm coming in now, sweetie."

The figure halted. Doug squeezed his eyes shut and opened them again, but the image in front of him was still a blur. Several seconds went by and neither moved. He shook his head back and forth at a rapid rate and tried to jolt back into reality. And then it occurred to him—whoever lurked there seemed too tall to be his pint-sized wife.

"Is that you, Candice?" he said. "Because I'm still not interested. I love my wife. You have to stop this—right now."

The figure shook its head but did not speak.

Candice was known in high school as the girl all the guys slept with, and being told no wasn't part of her limited vocabulary. Doug had resisted her for most of his senior year until one night when she showed up on his doorstep. It was like she knew he'd been left all alone. With his parents gone and Trista away at cheer camp, Candice pushed her way into his house. Doug tried to say no, he wasn't interested, but Candice tossed her head back and laughed while she unfastened the belt on her jacket, grabbed both sides and spread it all the way apart. Doug gasped. She was stark naked. She let the jacket drop to the floor and took her pointer finger and curled it back toward her. That was how she always got her man. She had the best body of any girl at school—one that none of the boys could resist—and she knew it.

Since the first day of the reunion cruise Candice had stalked him, showing up at the same excursions he was on with Trista and making obscene gestures whenever Trista glanced the other way. The mere sight of her made Doug's insides feel like they were on a continual roller coaster, and he just wanted to get off. On the second night, Candice had even cornered him in the hallway and slammed him up against one of the guest rooms. Doug had more than his fair share of drinks that night, but he'd managed to shove her off him before he stumbled down the hall to his cabin where Trista was waiting.

And now, there they were. Doug stared at the figure, sure it was Candice. She stood, silent, like she was waiting for something. *What kind of game is she playing now…*he thought? "It is you, Candice, isn't it?"

The figure shook its head and accelerated toward him, and for the first time in years, Doug wished he was in control of all his faculties. The figure wore a long black robe with a mask that looked like they'd just attended a masquerade ball with Marie Antoinette. Doug reached for the mask, but his hand swept the open air, not catching anything in its grasp.

"Who are you?" he said. "And what do you want?"

The masked person displayed a long, shiny object. Doug panicked. He tried to lunge to the side, but instead he stumbled backward, and the knife plunged into his chest. Doug's drink tipped from his hand and fell overboard into the icy depths below. Before he had time to react, he felt another sharp pain to his abdomen, and then another. He wanted to fight back, but he was drunk and helpless. The third jab cut deep, slicing straight to the heart, and as the life drained from his body and the blood spilled out, staining the deck below, he managed to utter one single word: "Why?"

The figure withdrew the knife from Doug's body, pulled him in close and whispered a single word—the last one he'd ever hear: *Revenge.* He pressed his hands into his gaping wounds and slumped over, trying to stand, but it was too late. Within seconds, Doug Ward was dead.

FIFTEEN MINUTES LATER

CHAPTER 2

If someone had asked me a year before whether I'd attend my twenty year class reunion, I probably would have said no. And yet, there I was, clad in a 1920's flapper costume with a smile welded on my face mingling with people who, for the most part, I no longer recognized. At first it was weird to see everyone, but as the week went by I realized I was glad I'd made the decision to relive the youthful bliss of my high school days.

The idea of taking a cruise to commemorate the anniversary appealed to everyone, about seventy percent of our graduating class showed up. And they were as shocked to see me as I was to be there. I looked around the room, staring into the diversity of faces. Some familiar, some I hoped to never see again, and others looked back at me like we'd been friends all our lives, and yet, I had no idea who they were.

Giovanni nudged me. "You were here a minute ago,

where have you gone?"

I turned to him and smiled. "Just thinking about how nice it is to be here—with you. And everyone else, but mostly you."

He leaned forward and our lips met. It didn't matter where we were when he kissed me or how often. I always got lost in the extra few seconds—the ones that turned a regular kiss into something much more meaningful.

"If you keep kissing me like that, we'll have to go back to the room," I said.

It was hard to determine what I found more attractive—the kiss or his vintage suit reminiscent of the days of Al Capone.

Going back to the room appealed to him. "I'm ready if you are."

"I never thanked you for coming with me," I said. "It's nice to have you here."

"It doesn't matter what I'm doing. I'll always make time for you."

"All right everyone," a voice shouted through the overhead speakers, "time to break in this dance floor for the evening." The woman made a swooping motion with her free hand. "Gather around people, don't be shy. Can we get our old prom king and queen out here to lead the way?"

To my left was Trista Ward, voted best everything a

person could be voted for in school: Best dressed, best looking, most popular. She set her glass of champagne on the table in front of her, spun around and frowned. "Doug was out on the deck a bit ago, let me grab him."

Several minutes went by with no sign of Trista or Doug. The music rattled on and on to the beat of an empty dance floor until Candice Flaherty stepped up. She pushed her way through all the costumed bodies, stepped forward and seized the microphone. She whipped her half-naked body around and faced the crowd. "Since those two lovebirds have decided to make us wait, how about we get the first dance started with the runners up?"

Someone in the crowd laughed and one person shouted, "Wouldn't that be you?"

"And Stephen…yes." Candice cupped her hand over her forehead and peered across the crowd. "You out there, Stephen? Don't be shy, now. I saw you earlier. Where are you hiding?"

"She's ah, an interesting one, isn't she?" Giovanni said.

I smiled. "It's probably not hard to see why we were never friends."

Stephen, who stood a few feet away from me, stepped forward with a look on his face that said he was more than happy to acquiesce her request. His wife, on the other hand, crossed her arms and huffed loud enough for the entire room to hear. Stephen faced her. "It's just one dance, honey. It'll be over before you know it."

She replied, "It's not the dance I'm worried about…it's that woman. She looks like she accepts singles on a stripper pole for a living!"

Stephen shook his head, "You have no reason to worry. She's just an old friend," and with that, he walked over and took Candice's outstretched hand. Other couples followed suit, and after a moment Paula Abdul's "Rush, Rush" blared through the speakers.

I glanced at Stephen's wife. Her arms were folded so tight she looked like she was being prepped to do time in a straitjacket. She glared at Candice like she wanted to glue her to the pavement on the freeway and commandeer the diesel truck that steamrolled over her trampy body.

"It's going to be okay," I said. "Candice flirts with all the guys, but she doesn't usually get anywhere. They all know what she's like."

She shrugged me off. "Yeah? You sure about that, because I've seen the way she's looked at *your* man all week."

"How's that?"

She winked. "Like he's next in line on the Candice-go-round, if you get my meaning."

"I'm not worried," I said.

She scoffed. "Honey, you should be."

Giovanni raised a brow and excused himself to refresh our drinks.

"Trust me when I say if Giovanni is interested in a woman like Candice Flaherty, he's got no business being with me," I said.

She shook her head and laughed and stuck her hand out. "I'm Rita."

"Sloane. Nice to meet you."

"So, I take it this is your reunion then?"

I nodded.

Rita grabbed her drink from the bar and took a generous swallow of what appeared to be a Long Island iced tea. A drink I never touched myself for fear I'd lose every sane thought to ever cross my mind. "Did you go to school with my Stephen?"

I nodded, again.

"I've always wondered what he was like back then," she said.

"Same guy he seems to be now," I said. "Nice. A little quiet, but a good guy."

"Still is...what about *her*?" she said with her finger pointed in Candice's direction. "What was *she* like?"

Girls like Candice had always been after one thing: Attention. She was loved by all the boys and hated by their girlfriends.

"We never ran in the same circles in school," I said, "but there were a lot of rumors back then about her, and none of them were good."

"Some people never change, and speaking of…" she said as she slammed her glass down on the counter of the bar, "I know a woman who has about two seconds to get her hand off my husband's ass before I remove it for her."

Rita lined Candice up in her sights and made a beeline through the crowd, shoving couples aside as she went. When she reached Candice, an argument ensued, and from the way Candice reacted, it was clear she thought the whole thing was funny—until Rita slapped her across the face.

Giovanni returned and handed me a drink. "I feel like I'm on one of those reality shows people watch nowadays," he said.

"Feels like high school all over again," I said. "And something tells me if Rita and I had gone to the same school, we would have been great friends."

CHAPTER 3

After Rita's one-woman show was over, she escorted Stephen, by the hand, out of the room like someone pulling a dog on a leash after he'd been scolded. At the same time, Trista walked in—minus Doug—with a look of concern on her face. She sized up everyone in the room and then bowed her head and stared at the floor.

I looked at Giovanni. "I'll be right back."

"Everything all right?"

"I'm not sure. Ask me again in five minutes."

I made my way over to Trista and said, "Are you okay?"

She shook her head. "I spoke to Doug earlier out on the balcony. He said he was only going to be out there for a minute and then he'd join me, but he never did."

I looked around. "Have you checked your room? Maybe he was tired and decided to call it a night."

"I've been there already—he wasn't there. The bed is still made up too. I don't think he's been back there since we left for dinner. Usually if he's had enough to drink for the night he goes back to our cabin and passes out on the bed, but…"

Candice sauntered across the room taking it upon herself to join our conversation. Her face was still bright red on one side from the embedded handprint that stung it several minutes earlier. "What's the matter, Tris—lose someone?"

"This doesn't concern you, Candice," Trista said.

"Doesn't it?"

"Don't think I haven't noticed what you've been up to all week."

Candice batted her store-bought eyelashes. "I have no idea what you mean."

Trista grimaced. "Do you really think I haven't noticed you making eyes at my husband since the moment we stepped on the boat?"

Candice put her hand over her mouth and laughed. "What a crazy accusation. There's nothing going on."

Trista put on a brave face, but her eyes were satiated with tears.

"I know there isn't," she said, her voice shaky. "And there won't be—not now, not ever."

Candice leaned over and whispered loud enough for both of us to hear. "Trista sweetie, if I wanted your husband, I would have already had him. Oops. I forgot. I have."

Trista surged forward. Her outstretched hands curled inward like a cat's paws, ready to strike. I stepped in between the two of them. "Get lost, Candice," I said. "Now."

Candice swirled her pointer finger at me and jabbed me in the chest with it. "Or what, Sloane? This doesn't involve you."

In that moment, my mind only processed one thing: Candice's fat finger pressed into me like she was the teacher and I was her student. I looked at Trista, "Wait here, I'll be right back," and then I grabbed Candice by the finger that penetrated my personal space and escorted her to the hall.

"Where's your room?" I said.

Candice smirked. "Like I'd tell you."

"Fine. Mine it is then."

I yanked her over to the elevator.

"Get your hands off me!" she said. "I'm not about to get in there with you."

She may have had the body back in the day, but I had the muscle. I shoved her in and pressed the button and the doors sealed shut. My hand remained affixed to her arm, and I didn't say a word while we ascended and then came to a halt on the fourth floor. Candice, on the other hand, let out her best scream. On a scale of one to ten, it was a three at best, and when the doors re-opened, it was still the two of us. I shoved Candice out and over to room 418 where I scanned my key card, opened the door and forced her inside. Once it was shut behind me, I wrapped my right arm around the front of her and hooked my left hand around her neck until I had her in a choke hold.

"Sloane, what the—why are you doing this to me!"

"Shut your mouth and listen. I know you get your kicks from messing with other women's husbands, but it stops…now. If I so much as see one of your eyeballs slant in the direction of another woman's man before this trip is over, I'll yank them from their sockets. Do you understand me?"

Candice sneered and went silent. I applied more pressure.

"Sloane…you're…choking…me."

"Nod if we have an agreement."

She moved her head what little she could and I let her go. "Good, now get out of my room."

Candice thrust her hands around her neck like I'd just broken it. "If I could just say—"

I pointed to the door. "I said get out!"

***

It took several minutes to bring myself back to center. Once I did I returned to the room where Trista was waiting. She had a confused look on her face. "What happened to Candice?"

I bobbed my shoulders up and down. "I'm not sure, but my guess is she won't return to the party tonight. Now let's get back to Doug. Any change?"

She shook her head.

"How long ago did you see him on the balcony?" I said.

"An hour ago, maybe."

"Could he be hanging out by the bar on one of the other decks or in the poker room?"

She shook her head. "He doesn't play card games, never has. And he told me he would be right in. He may fall short in some ways, but when he tells me he's going to do something, he's a man of his word."

I waved Giovanni over and gave him the I'll-fill-you-in-later look. "Trista's husband is missing. I'm going to help her search for him. If you want to go back to the room and wait for me, I'll join you as soon as—"

He placed a hand on my wrist. "What can I do to help?"

There were a total of six decks on the ship. After we walked to the photo section of the boat where all the pictures were displayed and Trista showed Giovanni what Doug looked like, the three of us split up and took two decks each. We made a plan to meet back in an hour regardless of whether we found him or not.

On my way out, Giovanni said, "Where do you think you're going?"

"On the balcony," I said, "like we just discussed."

"Not without this…"

He removed his suit jacket, wrapped it around me, winked and left the room.

"Your husband is easy on the eyes," Trista said. "And so thoughtful."

Heat generated around my face, and I wondered how many shades of red I'd turned. "Oh, he's not my husband," I said. "He's my, umm…we are, ah, he's my date. We're dating."

***

Forty-five minutes and two decks later, I'd found nothing but two teenagers getting frisky in the hot tub by the pool and a whole lot of people wandering around like happy hour had rocked steady for the past twelve hours. I wondered if Giovanni and Trista had better luck, but when I walked back into the atrium and saw the disappointed looks on their faces, I knew they hadn't found Doug either.

"Nothing?" I said.

Trista shook her head.

"Show me where you last saw him," I said.

"I'm not sure how that will help. It's so dark out, we won't be able to see anything. And anyway, he's not there now."

Giovanni walked over to the bar and summoned the man behind the counter. "Excuse me, my date thinks she may have lost one of her diamond earrings outside. I'm in need of a flashlight."

The man behind the counter nodded and called out to a kid that looked like a penguin in a purple vest. A few minutes later Giovanni returned, flashlight in hand, and the three of us headed outside. We walked about fifteen feet from the door and Trista stopped. "This is it," she said. "He stood against this railing."

"Are you certain?" I said.

She nodded. "I can tell because I remember him being by one of those round life preserver thingies."

Giovanni flicked on the flashlight and scanned the area. The light ran up and down the railing and then he stopped and glared at the deck for a few moments.

"What is it?" Trista said. "Did you find something?"

Giovanni gave me a strange look and then stared back at Trista. "I don't see anything out of the ordinary."

"Mind if I try?" I said.

Giovanni handed the flashlight over, but gripped it for a moment before letting it loose in my hand. It was then I realized he'd found something but didn't want to say what it was. I gave him a slight nod and knelt down and peered at the planks lining the deck next to where Doug had been standing. I didn't see anything at first, but then I noticed a series of splotches that looked like they'd been smeared. I leaned in to get a better look, and when I did, I was surrounded by what looked like dried paint. Only it wasn't. I was familiar with the particular shade of red, and it only came in one tint: Blood.

CHAPTER 4

"Neither of you see anything, are you sure?" Trista said.

I hated lying to her, but I didn't see the sense in causing her to worry until I figured out what had happened.

Trista braced herself against the railing and wound her fingers around it like she was holding on for dear life. I placed my hand on her shoulder. "You look exhausted. Why don't you go back to your room and rest for a while? Let us keep looking and see what we can find out, and I'll stop in and check on you in a bit."

"I can't," she said. "Not while Doug's out here somewhere. I'm embarrassed to say this, but he had a lot to drink tonight. I mean, he always does, but tonight he seemed more out of it than usual. It was like something triggered him. Maybe he couldn't remember how to get back to the room and he's in someone else's—"

Trista twisted up her face, and it was obvious what she was thinking—Candice hadn't returned to the party.

"I need to check on something," she said, and she walked back inside.

I turned to Giovanni. "Don't most ships have surveillance cameras these days?"

"This one would—yes."

"Good. I'm going to check into it. Will you keep an eye on her?"

***

It took about twenty minutes, but eventually I found a room set up with over a dozen miniature-sized televisions. The different screens offered multiple angles of the ship and refreshed at five-second intervals. I got closer and peeked through the small window for a better view. Two boys sat at a long desk that spanned the length of the room. One had nodded off, and the other was engrossed in a magazine—the kind most teenage boys hid between their mattresses so mom would never see. *Perfect.*

I twisted the knob and opened the door.

The boy with the magazine glanced up and then hurled it over to the corner of the room. When the magazine landed it sprawled open to a full page spread causing the boy's cheeks to light up like a motel sign on Hollywood and Vine. The other boy remained in his comatose state.

"Hey lady, you can't be in here."

"Oh, I'm sorry," I said. "Do you want me to leave?" I slipped off Giovanni's suit jacket and bent over an empty chair by the door giving him a front row seat to my rear view mirror. "I'm just so bored, and I saw you in here, and well—I thought you could tell me where I could go to have a good time."

His eyes widened like he'd just been given the keys to a brand new Ferrari. "What did you, umm, have in mind?"

I approached him and ran my fingers down the sides of my body, starting at my shoulders and working my way down to my waist and then rested them on my hips.

He swallowed—hard.

"What's your name?" I said.

"Toby."

I straddled the chair he sat in and lowered my body down until it rested on his lap. I pushed my face forward until it was level with his, leaned in and whispered, "What about you, Toby? Are you…busy?"

A bead of sweat trickled down his face as he tried his best to keep his eyes centered on me without looking down. After a few moments of consideration, he kicked the chair the other guy slept in and said, "Hey douche bag, wake up."

Douche Bag shouted an expletive and then rubbed his eyes. Once he got all the sand out and the view in front of him came into focus he said, "What the hell is she doing in here? Ma'am, I mean, lady—this room is restricted to the crew only." He looked back at Toby. "What were you thinking?"

Toby snapped his head back and laughed. "Dude, I'll give you a hundred bucks to take a hike for twenty minutes."

The other boy looked at him like he didn't understand why he said twenty when he only needed ten. He milled the moral dilemma around in his head and then got up and strolled out the door. Before it shut, he poked his head back in. "Twenty minutes—no more. Make it fast."

I slid off Toby and went to the door and locked it. When I turned back around he had his shirt off and was going for the belt on his pants at a rate faster than any heartbeat I'd ever heard in my lifetime.

I swirled my finger in the air. "No…no…no…not so fast."

"What do you mean? I thought you wanted to…?"

"These cameras," I said. "Do you ever see things you shouldn't?"

Toby laughed. "All the time."

"I want to see something first," I said. "Will you show me?"

"What's it worth to you?"

"Excuse me?" I said.

"I do something for you, you do something for me."

"Such as?" I said.

He indicated to my dress with his chin. "Take it off."

I took a moment to consider what he was asking and how far I was willing to go to get what I wanted. I'd been in a lot of compromising positions before, but nothing like the one I was in now. He requested my dress, not my bra and panties, so I rationalized it was no different than strutting around in my bikini on deck. With one hand I undid the back zipper and let my dress puddle around me on the ground. I stepped out of it and looked him in the eye. "Now will you show me?"

His eyes sparkled with anticipation. "What did you umm.. have in mind?"

I crossed the room, touching different screens as I walked like I was lighting up letters on *Wheel of Fortune.* "Can I just pick one?" I said.

He looked at his watch and sighed.

"We'll hurry," I said. "Promise. This is just so exciting!"

I selected a screen that displayed the various decks. "How does this work?" I said. "What if you wanted to look at one in particular instead of all of them in a rotation?"

"That's easy." He pushed some buttons on the keyboard in front of him and brought up the deck on level two.

"I was on level five tonight, and I'd love to see what was going on when I wasn't looking."

"Level five...let's see here." He pushed a couple more buttons and the level five camera sparked on.

"What time?"

"Around nine," I said.

"Which side?"

"The one by the dance floor."

When the screen refreshed I saw Doug, alive and staring out into a sea of nothing.

"All right, I showed you how it works; can we get back to you and me now? I wanna get the rest of those clothes off."

"In just a minute," I said. "I want to see where this guy goes."

He groaned. "Why do you care?"

I'd already fibbed more than a drug dealer in an interrogation room, what was one more?

"One of the women at the party was going around telling everyone she got it on with some guy out on the deck, and I wondered if it was true or not."

Toby stood up. "Why didn't you say so in the first place? Voyeurism—I like it!"

I tilted my head and smiled. "How about we fast forward to the good part?" I said. "Then we can get back to *us*."

He grabbed the remote, and the screen moved forward. After several minutes Doug's eyes shifted to the side and he spoke to a shadowy person shielded under a dark cloak.

Toby slowed things down until the recording played at regular speed and then stood up for a closer look at the coming attraction. "Hey, I bet this is it."

Somehow I didn't think so. The expression on Doug's face was not of a person prepared to enter the throes of passion—he looked scared.

"Wait a minute," I said. "Go back."

"Why?"

"Just do it."

He reversed until I told him to stop.

I put my finger on the screen. "What's that person holding in their hand?"

He shrugged. "This doesn't zoom, it just records."

I bent over the screen to get a closer look. The person talking to Doug held something in his right hand, but in black and white, it was too fuzzy to see. A knife?

"Play it again," I said.

Toby clicked the button, and we watched the person move toward Doug and then raise his hand and swing it down. Doug hunched over. Blood that appeared black on the monitor, oozed from his white button-up shirt. Toby threw his hand over his mouth and backed up until he tripped and fell over his chair. "This can't be happening. There's no way. How did I miss this?"

I had a pretty good idea. I continued to watch what

appeared to be a knife stab Doug again and again until he didn't move anymore. The cloaked person then tried to lift Doug but couldn't at first. The person rested a moment, looked around and then tried again. The second time Doug's body flopped halfway over the railing. He made no movement of any kind. A couple more heave-ho's and Doug's body plummeted over the side, tumbling to the water below. The cloaked person then threw the knife in after him. And Doug was gone.

I slipped back into my dress while Toby stumbled over to the phone and dialed. "This is Toby in the surveillance room. I need to talk to the captain." There was some chatter on the other end of the line and then Toby said, "I don't care if he's asleep. Wake him up—now!"

CHAPTER 5

I sat in a plain room with white paneling on all four walls and looked out the six foot windows at the lush green mountains of Jamaica. Mountains I'd hoped to explore, along with a nice, wet hike up Dunn's River Falls in my skivvies. Sadly, it was not to be. At the moment I was stuck with a bunch of men whose only interest was my role in the mysterious events that took place the night before.

The captain, upon learning a man had gone overboard, turned the ship around. He muttered something about how it was their obligation to return to the site and do a search and rescue. Because of the timestamp on the video surveillance camera, it didn't take long to make it back to the exact spot, but of course, there was no sign of Doug anywhere. And at that point, all kinds of red tape came into play. The way Giovanni explained it to me, because we were on the high seas and not on American soil or in American waters, it was hard to say what type of investigation would take place, and since the ship departed from a US port, special maritime jurisdiction applied. The only problem was, it often took a lot of finagling before anyone got anywhere.

"Jamaica can wait. This can't," the captain said. "Now…I want you to tell me again how you ended up in my surveillance room and why you wanted to see that footage."

He said the word *my* like a polygamist referenced one of his many wives.

"We've been over this," I said. "Twice. My story won't be any different now than it was fifteen minutes ago. I've told you everything."

"I still don't think you're giving me all of it. So let's go over it again," the captain said.

Giovanni, who sat back in the chair next to me with his arms crossed, leaned forward and chimed in. "I've allowed this to go on long enough. We have both complied with your repeated requests and your questions. Any further questioning is unnecessary at this point. We've done nothing wrong, and you have neither the right to question us or the authority to detain us any longer."

The captain bent over Giovanni's chair until he was mere inches from his face. "We'll sit here all day, but you *will* tell me whatever part of the story you two have left out."

I wanted to tap him on the shoulder and say: I wouldn't do that if I were you.

Giovanni remained calm. He pushed the captain away from him with his hand and said, "I need to make a call."

The captain threw his hands in the air. "This isn't jail. You don't get your one phone call. My boat, my rules."

Giovanni looked at me and said, "Say nothing more."

So I didn't. And aside from my stomach's disapproval of me skipping a nutritious breakfast, we sat in silence for the next twenty minutes.

When it was clear the captain's patience was spent, he said, "You two are behaving like you're waiting to get a lollipop from your mommy. Stop wasting my time. You're not getting a phone call."

In unison we shrugged our shoulders and continued to offer up the silent treatment. If he was going to ruin our day, the least we could do was return the favor. While we put up a united front, I played a mental list of songs inside my head to pass the time starting with Tom Petty's "I Won't Back Down" and ending with Twisted Sister's "We're Not Gonna Take It." By then, the captains face was so red it looked like one of his blood vessels was about to burst from his body, shoot across the room and smack both of us in the face multiple times.

With a great deal of reluctance, the captain looked at Giovanni and gestured to a phone on a desk. Giovanni clutched it in his hand and made his one phone call. He paused a moment and waited for the call to go through and then said, "Agent Luciana, please."

The captain's brow raised, but he said nothing.

Another pause and then, "How are you, Carlo? Yes, we've had a great time. I need your help with something."

From there, the details were explained to Carlo in a different language which I perceived to be Italian, and then Giovanni handed the phone to the captain. "He would like to speak with you."

The captain rolled his eyes, snatched the phone and positioned it over his ear. "Captain Manning here. Who's this?"

Those were the only words he got in before going mute for the next two minutes. Before he ended the call he said, "Yes, I understand." The phone was placed back on the receiver and the captain turned to Giovanni and frowned. "You could have told me your brother was FBI."

Giovanni smirked. "You didn't ask."

"Your brother has assured me the two of you will cooperate under his supervision if anything else is needed now or at any time in the future."

What the captain didn't know was Lucio answered to Giovanni.

"And?" I said.

The captain gritted his teeth. "I want to know your

whereabouts for the remainder of time you're on my boat, and I can assure you both, I will be watching. But for now, you're free to go."

I smiled. Maybe I'd get the chance to climb the river after all.

CHAPTER 6

Trista lay on the bed in her cabin curled up in the fetal position. When I walked in to check on her, she shot up and wrapped a blanket around herself. Her eyes were puffy, and her makeup, smeared. "So you saw him...go overboard?"

I nodded. "I'm so sorry. I wish I could have told you something else."

She closed her eyes. "I can't believe anyone could do such a thing. Doug was the kindest person. He wouldn't hurt anyone. Why would someone want to kill him? It doesn't make sense."

I leaned back on the desk behind me that was more suited for a child than an adult. This was the part of being a PI that I tried to shy away from, when a case I worked on became personal. It wasn't always easy to separate my feelings so I could focus on what I needed to: Finding out who killed Doug and why. And although this wasn't one of my cases, I couldn't sit back and do nothing. Doug and Trista were my classmates, and it didn't matter how many years had passed since high school or the fact that I'd barely kept in touch with anyone since I moved after my senior year; when something like this happened, it was like someone had attacked a member of my own family. And I wouldn't stand for anyone making a mess in my own backyard.

I boosted myself forward, sat next to Trista and patted her on the leg. Her body shook like it was undergoing some form of shock therapy treatment. I waited to speak until she seemed a little more relaxed which took some time and several minutes of sobbing and then drying her eyes and sobbing again.

"When you're ready, I'd like to ask you some questions. But if now isn't a good time…"

She shook her head back and forth. "What can you do…what can anyone do? Doug's dead. I don't even have a body to bury, and I probably never will. By now I bet he's not even in one piece. Did you know sharks can smell blood a quarter mile away? And once they catch a whiff, it's only a matter of minutes before…"

Tears gathered in the corner of her eyes and spilled onto the blanket she clutched in her hands. The only thing I could offer was to allow her to get it all out of her system. I felt powerless. I wanted to say something—anything, but it was times like these when I always felt I said the wrong thing.

I couldn't bring Doug back, but I could be there for her, and in that moment, my support was all that mattered to me.

When the tears had dried and gone, Trista glanced at me. "I'm ready. Ask your questions."

"Are you sure? Because we can do this later. I don't want to push you."

She pulled herself up to a seated position, threw the blanket to the side and wrapped her hands around her knees. "Tomorrow this will all be over. Let's do it now."

I nodded. "Can you think of anyone who wanted to harm Doug in any way?"

She shook her head. "Doug was the type of person who made friends, not enemies."

"What about his job? How were things there?" I said.

"I don't know. He didn't talk about it much. It's not like being the manager at TFB was hard. Granted the town has changed a lot since you were there last, but it's still small and friendly, just like it's always been."

"What about his demeanor? Have you noticed a change—anything out of the ordinary?"

Trista sat back and didn't say anything for a moment.

I leaned forward and looked her in the eye. "It's okay, you can talk to me. What you tell me stays in this room, between us. I'm not here to judge you, and if you want my help, I need to know everything."

"You remember what Doug was like in high school, right?"

"Who doesn't?" I said. "Every girl wanted to date him, and every guy wanted to *be* him. I was surprised when he turned down that football scholarship to Stanford and you two got married. The last time we talked, you guys had your bags packed and planned on attending together, but then you never left."

She nodded. "I was chosen to be on their cheer team, and we were all set, but right before we were supposed to leave, things got complicated."

"He threw it all away to become a bank manager for the rest of his life?"

She shrugged. "Once his mind was made up, he said he only cared about one thing—getting married."

"You two have been together a long time."

"Twenty years."

"What was married life like?"

She smiled. "Doug has always been sweet to me…."

"But?" I said.

"He had a drinking problem. It started right after we married."

"How bad was it?"

"It was tolerable at first, and I didn't think much of it. He'd come home from work and have a few beers. He seemed fine, and I figured he was a typical guy."

"What changed?"

Trista rubbed her arms with the palms of her hands like the air conditioning in the room had just been turned on and glanced out her balcony window. "I'm not sure I can talk about this."

In my experience as a PI I'd learned sometimes in order to get a person to a comfortable place where they were willing to talk, the best way to go about it was to share a personal experience of my own. It created a type of bond with the person and made them feel like not only did I sympathize, I empathized as well. But since I was a big fan of keeping my personal life private, I reserved this for special occasions only when I felt the risk would payoff in the end.

"Do you remember Colin Ross?" I said.

She squinted and stared at the television which wasn't on. "Vaguely. Wasn't he in our class?"

I shook my head. "He was one grade above us."

"Didn't he have a sister—Missy?"

"Mindy," I said. "I married Colin, right out of high school, just like you and Doug. Most people didn't know because I'd moved away that summer and we eloped."

"What does that have to do with anything?"

"Colin wasn't nice like Doug, and when he drank, he was even meaner." I stood up. "I want to show you something."

She bit down on the inside of her lip. "Okay."

I pulled my shirt up until it was level with the bottom edge of my bra.

Trista gasped and clasped her hand over her mouth. "What happened? Did someone—were you stabbed?"

I nodded. "My ex-husband had a drinking problem too. The only difference between him and Doug was Colin was a mean drunk."

"Mean enough to stab you?"

"A couple times," I said.

"Oh my gosh. Why?"

"I wanted a divorce, and he didn't."

"So…what did you do?"

Now it was my turn to pause and take a moment to think about how much more information I wanted to share. But I knew I needed to gain her trust. "I shot him," I said.

Her eyes widened like she'd been spit on by a gorilla at the zoo. "Are you serious?"

I nodded. "And then he lunged at me again with the knife so I shot him in his other kneecap. Let's just say he couldn't get around very well for a while. It was worth it. A week later he granted me the divorce I wanted."

"I'm sorry."

"I'm not. It was a long time ago, and I'm in a much better place in my life now. Look…my point in telling you all this is because I want you to know I understand what it's like to live with an alcoholic."

She fidgeted with her wedding ring, sliding it up and down her threadlike finger. "I tried to help him, I really did."

"Alcoholism can do a lot of things to a person," I said. "It was his responsibility to overcome it—not yours. It's a disease. You can't implicate yourself because of the choices he made."

"I guess somehow I always felt it was my fault, like he didn't stop because I didn't do enough to help him. I thought if I was a better wife, he wouldn't need to drink. If I was a better mother, he wouldn't need to drink."

I shook my head. "Alcoholism doesn't work that way," I said. "I'm sure you were an amazing wife."

Trista reached her trembling hand over to the nightstand and cupped it around a glass of water. She drew it close to her lips and took a sip. "Tomorrow this trip will be all over, and I have to go home and tell my kids what happened to their father. How am I supposed to look them in the eye and tell them?"

"Do Doug's parents still live in town?" I said.

She nodded.

"Talk to them first. Let them help you. You don't have to do this alone."

Her eyes glimmered with determination. "I know you

do some kind of PI work now, at least that's the rumor going around. I read it on the *Where Are They Now* paper displayed in the dining room. That's what you do, right?"

I nodded.

"Then I want to hire you."

I decided to spare her the details about not being licensed in the state of California. Besides, crossing state lines had never stopped me from snooping around before.

"Let me go home and get a few things squared away and then I'll fly down in a couple days. In the meantime, I'm going to leave you my number." I grabbed a pen off the counter, scribbled my number down on a pad of paper and handed it to her. "You can call me anytime; it doesn't matter when, I'll answer."

She stood up and grabbed her purse off the chair. "Do you want me to give you some money now, or can I pay you when you get in town?"

"Neither," I said.

She squinted, wallet in hand. "I don't understand."

"I don't want any money from you. Doug was a good friend to me once. I want to do this for both of you."

If I'd come from a family of huggers, I would have pulled her in close right then and told her what she needed to hear—I'd find the person who ended Doug's life, and everything was going to be all right. But the lack of affection

I'd been raised with left me with an inability to bond fully without feeling like I was being forced to sit through a long sermon in a sticky church with no air conditioning. So instead I reached out, patted her shoulder and let her know I'd call her the moment I arrived in town. It wasn't much, but it was something.

When I left the room I had the overwhelming sensation Trista was still keeping things from me. Maybe with time, she'd open up and lead me to Doug's killer without even knowing it. I wondered why Tehachapi's golden boy threw the chance of a great career away for little pay in a dead-end job. I wondered why he chose to spend his nights in a bar getting trashed when he had a family at home that loved him and parents who were the toast of town. Something drove him to the bottle, and I couldn't help but feel the key to the present lay in the past.

CHAPTER 7

"Earth to Sloane, come in," Maddie said. "Over."

I shifted positions on the sofa and sat up. "Sorry. I drifted again. I can't stop thinking about what happened on the boat and Trista and how she's doing."

"Have you heard from her?"

I shook my head. "Not a word. I called her last night, but she didn't pick up."

"How are you doing with all of it?"

"I'm anxious to fly down there and see what I can do to help," I said.

My eyes shifted to Lord Berkeley, a.k.a. Boo, who was fast asleep on the arm of my sofa.

"Why wait? Go. I'll take Boo to my house. It will be fine. Take all the time you need."

Upon hearing his name, Boo rose from the dead, hopped off the couch and trotted to the door. When I didn't get up fast enough, he scratched it with his paw a few times and then gave me a look that said: *Any day now.*

Maddie walked over and let him out and then back in about fifteen seconds later. Boo did several spins in a row and then hightailed it to the pantry and waited. Maddie bobbed her shoulders up and down and looked at me. "He didn't do anything. I don't get it?"

"It's the treats."

"What?"

"The new Beggin' Strips I got him," I said. "He thinks he can fake me out by going outside and doing nothing and still get a treat out of it. He goes to the door about twenty times a day now."

She laughed. "Time to get some new treats."

"No kidding."

Maddie bent down to give Boo a reward for the impeccable skill of going out the front door and coming back in. Her long blond pigtails with a splash of hot pink ink on the tips swooped down in front of Boo's face. He lifted his front paws and swatted her hair like he was trying to catch a fly with a single chopstick.

"Hey, stop that!" Maddie said. She looked my way. "Your dog is mental."

"He thinks you want to play."

She threw down another treat, sat back down on the couch and looked at me. "What happened on that reunion cruise of yours amazes me."

"I know, I still can't believe one of my old friends was murdered."

She shook her head and smacked me on the shoulder. "That's not what I meant. You tried to seduce a kid half your age. I didn't know you had it in you!"

I smiled. "There's plenty you still don't know about me."

She jabbed me in the ribs with her elbow. "Seems that way."

My phone rang.

"Who is it?" Maddie said.

I glanced down at the screen. "Trista." I pushed the button and a frantic Trista was already shouting before I could get any words out. "Trista, slow down," I said. "I can't understand you."

Her words ran together like a run-on sentence. The only thing I could make out was something about Rusty Jenkins being attacked outside Flex It, the town gym.

"How badly was he hurt?"

When she replied the phone slipped from my hand and plummeted to the carpet. I bent down and picked it up in time to hear her say, "Sloane, are you still there?"

The only thing I could mutter was, "I'll be there in the morning. Everything's going to be okay…I'm coming."

Maddie's face filled with concern. "I know that look."

"Another one of my classmates was just found outside the local gym."

"Found what? Passed out because his workout was too intense?"

I shook my head. "Stabbed. He's dead."

CHAPTER 8

The last time I stepped foot in my hometown of Tehachapi, California had been for my aunt's funeral several years earlier. At that time, it surprised me how much the town had changed in the years since my move to Park City, Utah. To return and see all the differences was like running into an old boyfriend who'd been voted Best Hair in school, beating out all the guys *and* the girls, and then finding time had left him not just with a bald spot, but bald all together. This type of thing might have been acceptable had the old boyfriend entered the UFC or was blessed with a name like Bruce Willis, but if he was skinny and had a square-shaped head, well, it just wasn't the same thing. And that's what Tehachapi had become to me—different, almost to the point of indistinguishable. Whether it was different bad or different good had yet to be determined.

I entered town on Highway 58 and was amazed to find my aunt's old billboard still hoisted up twenty-something feet in the air on the right-hand side of the road.

The town had commissioned the painting when I was in high school. She'd divided it into four sections, one for every season of the year. Each section reflected something different: The mountains, a sprawling orchard with rows and rows of fruit trees, the windmills, and of course, the snow. Back then the sign had read:

>WELCOME TO TEHACHAPI
>LAND OF FOUR SEASONS

What the sign said back then was true, and the locals joked that not only was the town capable of four seasons, but all four could be experienced in the same day. Twenty years of weather like that tarnished the sign which no one had bothered to maintain. It bent inward, the wood had split and chipped away sections of paint, and the sun had produced a magic fading act. Now all that remained was:

>TO TEHACHAPI
>LAND OF FOUR

Time for a new sign.

I veered off the exit onto Tehachapi Boulevard and drove several blocks until I reached Peach Street.

Trista was outside on the porch when I drove up sporting a ball cap and dark sunglasses and leaning on her mailbox for support. "I'm glad you came," she said when I exited the car. "I didn't think you'd get here so fast."

Thanks to Giovanni's private plane, nothing was out of my reach. "I just wish it wouldn't have taken something like this to get me here."

She motioned for me to follow her with her hand. "The kids are still at school. Come inside and we can talk."

I followed her through the door and removed my shoes. She turned and said, "Do you need anything? Water? Soda? I think I have some Diet Pepsi in the fridge."

Before I could respond I felt something hard brush beneath one of my feet. I flew forward and grabbed the corner of the wall to brace myself so I wouldn't go down.

Trista scrunched up her nose like she'd just found something old in the fridge. "You don't have any kids, do you?"

"What makes you say that?"

"The way you tiptoed your way around the room when you walked in here like you thought a grenade would go off."

I looked at the reddened area beneath my foot and tried to push through the pain like it was nothing. "How many do you have?"

"Kids?"

I nodded.

"Three."

She pointed to a collage of photos on the wall. There were two boys who appeared to be twins and one girl who was much older. "My two boys, Joshua and Jack, are six, and my daughter, Alexa, just turned twenty. She's at Stanford. Top of her class. She wants to be a doctor. In a lot of ways she's living the life I never had."

"Do you see her much?"

She shook her head. "It's been about a month now, but she'll be home this weekend. You'll have to come for dinner so you can meet her."

The age difference between the girl and the two boys shocked me, but I tried to keep a straight face. I looked at the photo of the girl again. Blond hair and blues eyes which were odd considering both Trista and Doug had brown hair and brown eyes, the same hair and eye color as their two sons.

Trista forced a smile. "Why don't we sit at the table?"

I pulled out a chair and started to lower myself into it until Trista said, "Hold on! Don't sit there."

A soggy, partially-wet substance was stuck to the slats of the chair and appeared to be the remnants of some type of fruity oatmeal left over from that morning. Trista snatched a rag from the counter and wiped it down. When she finished, she threw the rag into the sink and grasped the sides of the kitchen counter with both hands. She closed her eyes and stood there, breathing deeply to calm herself.

I sat in the chair and tried to think of what I could say to make it all better, even though I knew nothing I said could change anything. "You have beautiful children. I've always wanted kids."

She opened her eyes and spun around. "Why don't you have any?" And then her hand flew over her mouth. "I'm sorry, how rude. I didn't mean to be so intrusive."

I shook my head. "It's okay. I mean, it's not something I talk about much, but I wasn't ever able to get pregnant."

She sat in the chair beside me. "It took almost fifteen years to conceive my twins."

"You mean after you had your daughter?"

She stiffened. "Umm, yeah. After Alexa was born, getting pregnant wasn't easy like I thought it would be."

I'd done the math in my head and figured out that their daughter had to of been born right after they graduated high school—an obvious reason to get married. I wondered if that led to their sudden change in plans, but I sensed there was a lot more to it.

Trista studied my face for a moment like she knew I was milling the possibilities over in my mind. "It's a long story. Let's save it for another time, okay?"

I nodded. "You know what I don't understand? Why

didn't Doug go into the family business? His parents are the richest people in town."

"Yeah, but they don't get along very well. They nose into our lives enough as it is, trying to throw their money at us and influence every decision we make, but Doug made sure we always had a degree of separation. If not for that, we never would have survived here."

It made sense.

"Tell me more about what happened last night with Rusty."

She folded her arms and leaned back in her chair. "All I know is he'd gone to the gym like he does almost every night. When he was finished working out, he went out to the parking lot and someone had moved his bike."

"His *bike*?"

"Harley-Davidson."

"How do you know someone moved it?"

"My neighbor's husband was there and said they'd finished their workout at the same time and walked out together. That's when Rusty noticed his bike wasn't where he parked it. My neighbor was in a hurry to get home, so he left. About twenty minutes later Rusty was found in a grassy area next to the side of the building, dead."

"And his bike?"

She shrugged. "Sorry, that's all I know."

I reached into my bag, pulled out a bottled water, unscrewed the lid and took a sip. Trista's eyes shifted to a calendar hanging on the wall next to her. She gazed at it like she wished she would have taken it down before I got there. The top portion had a picture of a waterfall. It was made on flimsy paper and reminded me of the kind of token gift passed out at banks each year. On it were a series of various appointments for the month. Under today's date there were three words written so small I could hardly make them out. I leaned over and pretended to stare at a floral arrangement on a pedestal next to the calendar and then snuck a peek at the writing in the square box. It said: AA 7 p.m.

Interesting.

"You said Rusty was stabbed—once or repeatedly?" I said.

"Once in the chest from what I heard."

We sat in silence for a moment, then Trista said, "What are you thinking?"

In my experience, when a person died as a result of being stabbed, the motive was always personal. The knife created a type of one on one with the victim, and often, that type of attack carried a lot of pent up rage with it. But, I wasn't ready to speculate with Trista.

"Whoever attacked him had to be precise for him to die from a single wound. Doug and Rusty were pretty chummy in high school, right?"

She nodded. "They played football together, and for a while Rusty dated my best friend. But after we graduated we didn't hang out much."

"What happened?" I said.

"Life. Doug became a family man, and Rusty opened a tattoo shop. He tried to come around, asked Doug to come to a few poker nights with some of the other guys, but Doug was weird about it."

"In what way?" I said.

"All I know is, he didn't want anything to do with those guys."

Two deaths within days of each other, both men stabbed. Doug and Rusty may not have been close anymore, but there was definitely a connection—there had to be.

CHAPTER 9

The parking lot at Flex It was empty except for a few vehicles and one squad car minus the presence of any officers. I exited my rental car and was yanked backward by someone who shielded both my eyes with his hands like I was the counter in a game of hide and seek.

"Well, well...Sloane Monroe. You've managed to stay away so long I assumed I'd never see you again," a male voice said. The voice was rough but had an unmistakable high-pitched squeak that rounded out the end of his sentences.

"You should remove your hands so I can see who I'm talking to," I said.

"Awww, come on. You don't recognize my voice?"

"How'd you know I'd be here?"

He laughed. "It's not like there are millions of people in this town."

Beads of sweat beneath his fingers seeped an oily moisture that melded with my skin and spread, and I had the sudden urge to scrub every layer until the layer of grime he transferred peeled off. He was too close, and I didn't know how long I could withstand his advances.

"Seriously, Jesse. You can let go now."

Most girls at some point in their high school years always had what I liked to call 'restraining order guy'—the one who never went away no matter what you did or how hard you tried. Jesse was the equivalent of that to me. He was the kind of person who seemed harmless but followed me around like a hitchhiker in need of shelter in the middle of a snowstorm.

Jesse peeled his hands off me and spun me around, but before I could get a good look at him, all I could see were his moistened lips attempting to acquire a landing position on mine. As his tongue protruded out of his mouth in an attempt to pass first base, I whipped back and swung my hand in his direction.

He rubbed his cheek and frowned. "What the—why'd you do that? I was just trying to say hello."

Hello? Is he serious?

"We're not eighteen anymore, Jesse. You don't try to suck the life out of a person you haven't seen in twenty years."

He took a step back and muttered something under his breath that sounded like 'you haven't changed much.'

"What was that?" I said.

"Nothin'. It wasn't anything."

"What kind of cop behaves like that anyway?" I said.

He smiled and in a flash was back to himself again. "The romantic kind."

In the looks department, Jesse was the perfect example of what time could do for a person. The once skeletal, acne-faced boy had turned into a man with flawless skin and a slim body worthy of the cover of *GQ* magazine. If only his personality had changed along with the rest of him.

"Why weren't you on the reunion cruise last week?" I said.

"I was."

I shook my head. "I never saw you."

"I was busy."

"There were plenty of class soirees to attend during the week; I didn't see you at any of them," I said.

"Yeah, well, the poker tables were calling my name."

"Every day? You couldn't come out of hiding to say hello?"

"I saw *you*. Several times, in fact. But you were always too caught up with the dude you were with to notice there was life going on around you."

"That's not—"

"Why are you here, Sloane?"

I shrugged. "I had some free time, and after the cruise I thought—why not come for a visit?"

He shook his head. "Your eye twitched."

"What?"

He took his finger and pointed it at my left eye. "In school your eye always twitched when you were feedin' me a line of bullshit."

That isn't true, is it?

He leaned against the door of my car, folded his arms and slanted his head to the side. "Try again."

I wasn't in the mood to play games, and it was obvious he was keeping me from nosing around at the crime scene. "Can you move? I need to go."

His backside remained glued to the door. "Why? You just got here. Were you plannin' on gettin' a workout in, or did you have an uh, more sinister idea in mind?"

"Get out of my way, Jesse. I mean it."

He didn't budge.

"Trista told me you were here."

I stepped back. "So you know?"

"You're helping her find the person who supposedly murdered Doug? Yep."

I'd forgotten how hard it was for people in small towns to keep their mouths shut.

"And what, you showed up to tell me to mind my own

business and offer me a personal escort off the property?"

He laughed. "Naw. I'm here to ask you to dinner."

"What?"

He leaned forward, shoved his fingers through the belt loops on both sides of my jeans, and yanked my body toward him until our waists were pressed against each other. "Have dinner with me, Sloane."

I wrapped my hands around his wrists and pulled back, but it was to no avail. "Let go."

"You're not the only one who wants to know what happened to Doug. He was my friend too."

"You, Doug, Rusty, and Nate. The four of you were like your own little version of the Rat Pack in school and now two of the four are dead. Coincidence?"

"Look, you have questions, I might have answers. Did ya ever think of that?"

I doubted it. "I'm busy tonight," I said.

"How 'bout tomorrow night?"

His tight grip on me combined with the rancid odor of his over chewed piece of citrus gum gave me the urge to teach him a lesson he'd never forget, but I resisted. I needed answers, and it was worth a couple hours to find out what he knew—if anything. "Dinner. And it's not a date."

"I know, you've got a boyfriend…for now."

CHAPTER 10

At seven pm I walked into the Tehachapi Cultural Center and sat in the middle of a semi-circular row of chairs. Men and women flanked both sides of me. Some smiled and gave a curious nod; others avoided direct eye contact altogether and gazed at the floorboards, their shoes, and any object that allowed them to pass the time in silence without any verbal exchanges. If there was a mood to the room, it was a somber one.

After a few minutes, a man emerged from the corner of the room where he'd been in deep conversation with a long blond-haired woman. He stood at a wooden podium that looked like it belonged in front of a casket at a funeral home. "You've all probably heard by now a member of our group was killed on the class reunion cruise several days ago," he said. "I'd planned to read from the *Big Book* tonight and follow our regular course like usual, but many of you were good friends with Doug, and out of respect for his passing, I thought you might like to share a few of your thoughts and memories first."

A man a couple chairs to my left raised his hand. The speaker at the podium tilted his head toward him to indicate his request was granted. The man relayed a story about how Doug had given him a loan at the bank after every other bank in town turned him down. Similar comments floated around the room until almost every person had their say.

While I sat and listened my eyes veered back to the blond woman who sat silent, disengaged from the conversation going on around her. The woman's thumb and pointer fingers were pressed beneath her eyelids like she was trying to form some kind of invisible shield, but it didn't hide the fact she was crying. Tears dripped over her light pink fingernails and ran down the backside of her hand until it was almost completely soaked.

A minute later, the blond woman stood up, turned to the man at the podium and whispered, "Excuse me, I need to go," and then she bolted for the door. I followed.

When she reached the parking lot, I broke my silence. "Are you all right?"

She pivoted on her black suede boot and squinted. "Why are you following me?"

"I wasn't. I mean, I guess I was, but I saw how upset you were in there and—"

"Who are you? I know everyone in this town, but I haven't seen you before. People don't just pass through and poke their head in on an AA meeting, so what are you doing here?"

"I'm an old friend of Doug's from high school."

She dried her eyes with her hand and shook her head. "You couldn't be."

I shrugged. "Why?"

"Because if you were, I'd know you."

"What's your name?" I said.

"What's yours?"

"Sloane."

We both stood there while her brain ran a scan of all prior Sloane's she may have known in her life. And then, a recollection. "Is your last name Monroe?"

I nodded and she rushed over and threw her arms around me. My arms remained at my side—stiff and wishing for immediate release.

"I can't believe this!" she said.

I couldn't believe it either. I patted her on the back a couple times and tried to understand why she'd latched on to me. She pulled back after a minute, rested her palms on my shoulders, and tipped her head to one side. "Wait. You don't recognize me, do you?"

"I'm sorry, no."

She let me go, stepped back and pointed at herself. "I'm Heather Masterson."

Still nothing.

Her eyes lit up. "Remember that time in school when you came around the corner and found me in the trash can?"

I flashed back to a memory from my senior year of a scared young girl with a mouthful of tinsel teeth. "Some of the varsity girls put you in there as part of freshman orientation."

She laughed. "Yeah, they spilled that plate of spaghetti on my head too. You helped me out and gave me one of your sweatshirts from your locker since mine was soaked in red. I idolized you after that."

"You were a few years younger than we were. I didn't think you knew Doug very well back then. Did you meet in AA?"

She nodded. "I was his sponsor."

"But I thought sponsors—"

"Had to be the same sex? They probably prefer it, but there weren't enough of us, and it's not like there's a rule against it. Doug chose me, and I didn't want to say no."

"What do you mean—chose?"

"He'd come to a few meetings and heard me talk about how long I'd been sober and said he was moved by my story of sobriety and by what I shared with the group. After that he asked me to be his sponsor."

Heather rubbed her hands up and down her bare arms. "Do you, ah, drink coffee? There's a great place around the corner if you don't have any plans."

I smiled. "Your car or mine?"

***

The diner was closed when we got there so we opted for hot beverages from a metal dispenser at a gas station and sat in my car with the heater on high.

"Have you been to AA before?" she said.

I shook my head. "First time."

"It's a great group. You'll like it."

"Actually, I'm not umm…"

She reached out her hand and pressed her fingers into my arm. "It's okay…I know how you feel. It's always hard the first time. The good thing is you took a step today that will change your life."

I felt too guilty to continue the farce any longer, especially when she was a recovering alcoholic herself. "I don't have a drinking problem."

Her face twisted into ten different kinds of confused before she said, "You don't have to deny it any longer. Once you attend a few more meetings you'll realize we're like the family you never knew you had, and now that you have us, we'll always be here."

"No listen," I said, "I wasn't there because I have a problem."

She shook her head like she still didn't believe me. "Why else would you go?"

"How long were you Doug's sponsor?" I said.

"A few months. He said he'd been trying to come for years, but it's not easy. If you can make it through the door and face your friends and neighbors, it's considered a big deal, especially in this town."

"I wonder what made him commit."

"Trista."

"She made him go?"

Heather shook her head. "She'd started taking med's. I guess that reality gave him the push he needed."

I took a sip of my drink and set it down in the cup holder. "Why?"

"Doug said she was depressed. He blamed himself and thought if he could stop drinking, maybe she'd start to care again."

"What made him think she didn't?"

Heather shook her head. "I don't know what kind of dose they had her on, but it was high enough to make her behave like she was in a coma. He'd come home and she hadn't made dinner like she usually did, the house was a mess, the twins had destroyed the place…"

"And where was Trista while all this was happening?"

"In bed most days with the door locked behind her. The kids basically fended for themselves."

"You seem to know a lot about their situation," I said.

She shrugged. "I guess."

"Do all sponsors get this involved in their partners personal life?"

Heather scratched behind her ear. "He needed someone to talk to, and I was there."

"Well then, it was good he had you for a friend."

She placed her coffee cup on the center console between us. "Yeah, I guess that's why I got so emotional in there."

"If you two were so close, maybe you can tell me why you think he's dead," I said.

"Whoa—what makes you think I know?"

I wiggled my arms up and down. "You seem to know everything else."

"I was shocked when I found out what happened. Everyone loved Doug."

"I've heard that a lot lately," I said, "but at least one person didn't feel that way."

"I don't understand what you mean. I was told he got drunk and fell over the railing on the ship."

I shook my head. "I was there, on the boat. I saw the surveillance camera. He didn't fall over the side; he was stabbed and then thrown over."

She clasped her hand over her mouth and flicked her head from side to side. "Rusty died from a stab wound too, didn't he? I can't believe it. What does it mean? I don't understand what's happening."

Heather stuck a couple fingers in her mouth and bit down.

I looked away.

"I know I shouldn't," she said.

"What?"

"Bite my nails. Can't help it. I always do it when I'm nervous. Sometimes I bite them down so far, they bleed."

I turned back around and was glad to find her hands in her lap again. "Is there anything that connected Doug to Rusty over the past year?"

"Nothing. They were opposites in every way. Everyone in town adored Doug, but people always had some kind of beef with Rusty."

"Over what?"

She rolled her eyes. "Everything. Rusty didn't have the best temper. Most people around here just tried to stay out of his way."

I thought back to all the suspensions he received as a

teenager for fist fights. "I remember what he was like when we were younger."

"Take high school and multiply by five and you'll get the man Rusty turned into after he graduated." She turned her body to the side and faced me. "Wait—is that why you're here? The murders? Are you involved?"

"I'm curious about what really happened to my old friend. Aren't you?"

She nodded.

"Good, so if there's anything else you can tell me…"

"I thought I already did."

It was about to get real. From the moment our backsides slid into the leather seats of my rental car, I'd watched her—her hand gestures, her body movements, the way her eyes flickered to the side whenever something I said pressed her uncomfortable button. Over the years I'd learned it wasn't always what people said that gave me the answers I was seeking, it was what they didn't say.

"So far you've only told me what you wanted me to know," I said. "What I'm interested in is what you're not saying."

She frowned. "I don't know what you mean."

"You're lying to me."

"About what?"

"Your relationship with Doug."

She squeezed her hands together like she wished a higher power could teleport her out of the car, scoop her onto a magic carpet and whisk her away.

"Care to know what makes me think you're keeping something from me?" I said.

She didn't respond.

I grabbed the cup from the center console and held it out in front of her. "Two things. You set this cup in between us. Now, I know that doesn't seem like much, but you did it right after I used the word *friend.* It bugged you."

"You got all that from a cup?"

"Did you know that sometimes when a person is lying they'll place something between themselves and the other person? It's like a miniature barrier you and your lies can hide behind. You probably weren't even aware you were doing it, but I was. And before that you scratched behind your ear. We could sit here all night and I can keep going—it's up to you."

She blinked her eyes in disbelief.

"Heather—whatever it is, you can tell me," I said, "and you should, tell me. You don't have to keep it inside anymore. Doug's dead and he's not coming back."

She flattened her hand and rammed her head into it a few times the way a person did when they'd made a mistake they couldn't take back. "I slept with Doug, all right!"

I leaned back in my seat. Now we were getting somewhere. "How many times?"

"Once. It didn't happen right away, and it shouldn't have ever happened. He trusted me, and I let things go too far between us. But I swear I didn't know anything about anyone wanting to harm him. And I knew we shouldn't have slept together, but I couldn't help it. The closer we got, the more I fell for him."

"Did Doug feel the same way?"

"I don't know—I don't think so. Doug always talked about how much he loved his wife. I was more of a friend for him to confide in. He even cried afterward saying Trista deserved to know what we'd done, and he had a hard time looking her in the eye which further complicated their relationship."

Usually I was an advocate for complete honesty between a man and a woman, but Doug was dead. The truth would only make things worse. "It would be for the best if you kept your little indiscretion to yourself. Losing Doug has been hard enough on Trista. I'm glad she never found out about you two."

Heather stared out the window and choked back her tears. "That's just it. She did."

CHAPTER 11

The crisp mountain air breathed life into a new morning. I sat up, peeled back the thick tapestry that adorned the hotel window and peered out into the courtyard. A man was swimming laps in the pool a few stories below. His chest was whiter than the tips of my fingernails, and he was in desperate need of a jacket.

I thought about Heather's confession the night before and wondered why Trista kept it from me. But what woman wanted to admit her husband cheated on her to someone they hadn't talked to in twenty years? That kind of information wasn't exactly the best ice breaker. *Hi, nice to see you again after all this time…hey, did you know my husband is responsible for putting the U in unfaithful?* It made me wonder what else she hadn't told me.

I showered, placed a call to Giovanni, and took the elevator down to the lobby where I feasted on a complimentary bagel and peach yogurt. Not the hearty breakfast I had in mind, but it would keep me going for a few hours. I finished and headed outside. When I got to the parking lot I took one look at my car and realized it had been altered from its former state of unblemished perfection. All four tires had been slashed with excellent efficiency by someone who wasn't a virgin when it came to wielding a knife.

An employee of the hotel wheeled a bin of trash past me. He lifted his chin and smiled and then took one look at my tires and ditched the trash can to run inside. I followed.

When I caught up to him at the front desk I said, "You don't need to call anyone, I can handle this myself."

He shook his head. "The hotel manager already notified the police. Someone's on their way over. You should wait here."

"I need to grab something from my room," I said.

He started to say 'wait', but it was too late. I was already up the stairs and didn't bother looking back. I whipped the key card out of my jean pocket and sprinted toward my room. When I turned the corner two maids stood there, one with her finger aimed at the center of my door. She then threw her hands up in the air and spoke a bunch of gibberish to the other woman whose eyes popped open about three times their normal size.

Mounted to my door was a plain white piece of paper

that had been ripped in half, but that wasn't what their eyes were riveted on. It was the sharp object used to secure the note in place.

I shooed them away with my hand and leaned in for a closer look. The object was small and delicate. It reminded me of something a surgeon would wield over a patient in the operating room. I pulled out my phone, snapped a photo and texted it to Maddie along with the words: I'LL EXPLAIN LATER. Then I shifted my eyes to the note. The handwriting was sloppy and careless:

THIS DOESN'T CONCERN YOU.
STAY OUT OF IT AND YOU WON'T GET HURT.

The problem with notes like this was I never had the chance to reply, which I considered a pity. I would have said:

IT'S NOT ME THAT NEEDS TO BE WORRIED.
IT'S YOU.

I wanted to yank the knife out and get a better look at it, but something told me the maids wouldn't keep quiet, and I didn't need the Tehachapi Police Department offering me an escort out of town before I tracked down Doug and Rusty's killer.

I turned to the maids. "Did you see who did this?"

They looked at me with a blank stare that made me regret all those years I flirted with Troy Lassiter instead of paying better attention in Spanish class. The only thing I *did* remember from back then was my teacher saying, "Cual es la fecha de hoy?" But I didn't see how them giving me the date would help the current situation any. Given the language barrier, I did the only other thing that came to mind. Charades. I balled my hand into a fist and thrust up and down like I was doing a reenactment of the shower scene in *Psycho* and then moved my arms like a senior citizen power walking in the mall in the wee hours of morning. I hoped my one-woman show would indicate someone stabbing the note on the door and then fleeing the scene. I thought about saying 'capiche', but realized I would further confuse them by adding yet another language to the mix.

When my performance was finished, I smiled, proud in my ability to get my message across without the use of actual verbiage. I looked at both women and waited for the results. One of the maids grabbed the shirt of the other and they fled in terror, leaving their cart of goodies behind. Excellent. I knew I'd missed my calling as an award-winning actress.

With the maids gone and no cops in sight, I decided whoever left the message was long gone, but it still wouldn't hurt to have a look. I stuck my key card into the slot, traded my cell phone for the 9mm in my handbag and raced back down the hall toward the stairs. There were three floors below me and I scaled them all, but the corridor was vacant all the way down. I was too late. The walls around me offered nothing but silence. If someone had been there, they were long gone.

I climbed back up the stairs, pushed the door open and rammed it into something on the other side.

"What are you trying to do, maim me?" Jesse said.

"How was I supposed to know you were behind the door?"

Jesse rubbed his nose with his hand, but his eyes were fixated on my gun. "What the...where'd you get that?"

"Same place you got yours probably."

He stuck his hand out. "Not funny. You can't run around here with that thing."

"I have a license."

"And you think that allows you to whip it out whenever and wherever you please?"

I slid by him without a word and went straight for my room.

Jesse followed so close behind I could hear the shift in his pant legs as he walked. "So," he said, "who'd you piss off?"

I reached my door and noticed the note and its accompanying knife-like object were no longer stabbed into the middle of it. All that remained was a small nick in the wood. I spun around and glared at Jesse. "Where are they?"

He angled his head in the direction of my room and it dawned on me my door was cracked open. I shoved it all the way back and walked in. A second officer was standing in the middle of the room looking around.

"Excuse me," I said, "you don't have any right to be in here. The note was *on* my door not in my room."

He exchanged looks with Jesse but didn't say anything. The knife and the note rested on the desk packaged in separate plastic bags. The police officer had his hands cupped over one another like he was concealing a small bird, but the shiny piece of pink plastic that emanated from his hand was unmistakable.

I leaned forward and held my hand out. "What the hell are you doing with my cell phone?"

No response. Jesse jerked his head and the officer handed it back to me.

I held my phone out to Jesse and shook it. "What the hell was he doing with my cell phone!"

Jesse sighed and glared at the officer. "Walker, wait for me outside please. And not in the hallway, in the SUV."

"But don't we need to—"

Jesse shook his head. "Just do it. Now."

The other guy nodded and walked out. Jesse leaned

his weight against the door, creating a barrier between me and the officer.

"I'm not going to attack him if that's what you're worried about," I said. "I just wanted him to answer the question. He's been in my room with his mitts all over my things."

Jesse stepped forward and placed his hand on my shoulder. I shrugged it off. The smell of cheap aftershave permeated the room. "Come on now, Sloane," he said. "Don't be like that. I'll talk to him about the phone."

My eyes darted around my room from the bed, to my nightstand, and then to the counter by the bathroom door. "It wasn't just my phone—my clock isn't in the same position. Neither are my clothes. You two aren't detectives, you're beat cops, which means it isn't customary for you to go through my things."

"Look, I'm sorry he was in here, okay? He wants a promotion—bad, so he looks for any way he can get it. He's just tryin' to be thorough. I've got him under control. Can we move on?"

I rubbed my forehead with my hand and sat on the edge of the bed. Jesse followed my lead and sat so close I could almost breathe in his breath when he breathed out. I scooted over.

He placed his fingers on the nape of my neck and rubbed in a circular motion while he scooted back over until his hip touched mine. "You need to relax."

As much as his hand movements relieved the tension I felt, I couldn't allow it. I stood up. "Stop, Jesse…you can't."

He tried to grab my hand but I jerked it away. Undeterred, he attempted it a second time. "Come on now, you don't need to run away from me."

I walked over to the desk and leaned against it. "Have you asked the hotel manager for the security tapes?"

He laughed. "Uh, there aren't any. Not here anyway."

"What kind of hotel doesn't have security cameras?"

"In case you missed it Sloane, this isn't the Ritz-Carlton."

I threw my hands up in the air. "Great."

"Someone is on the way over to dust the door and your rental car for prints. Until then, I need you to hang out with me until we can get you a room somewhere else."

I shook my head, shoved my gun into my bag and walked out the door.

"Sloane, you're not going anywhere. You can't."

Can't?

"I feel cooped up in here. I need to be outside…free from all this," I said. "Trust me, you don't want to see what happens if you force me to sit here."

"Fine. Stay close and leave the gun."

I glanced at my gun which was now back inside my bag and looked at Jesse on my way out the door. "Not a chance."

CHAPTER 12

"You don't understand, Maddie. They were in *my* room, with their hands on *my* possessions, touching *my* stuff! And they moved things around, I could tell, and I—"

"Slow down…when's the last time you took something?"

"Ate something?"

"No…."

"For what?"

"Your anxiety, sweetie."

I sighed. "I'm fine."

Maddie made a noise that sounded like 'phooh.'

"What was that?" I said.

"Gum. If I chewed it any longer it would have disintegrated in my mouth. Listen, I know you think you're fine, but you're not. I can hear it in your voice. I know how you get when you're out of your element, and believe me, you're not just a little out this time."

"I can handle it. If Jesse could just keep his hands to

himself—"

"Who's Jesse?" she said.

"A guy I knew when I used to live here," I said. "He's a cop now. It seems like every time I show up somewhere, he does too."

"Where are you now?"

I looked around and realized I'd walked about a block away from the hotel. The smell of melted butter and vanilla wafted through the air. I stopped and breathed it in until I spied the location it came from.

"I went outside to get away from Jesse," I said. "How's Boo?"

"Let's just say OCD runs in your household."

"What do you mean?" I said.

"Did you know your dog separates his food by flavor? All the dry chicken pieces are rejected. He removes them out of the bowl with his mouth and makes a pile on the floor next to him until all that's left are red ones."

"What can I say," I said. "We're a red meat kind of family."

"Have you talked to Giovanni yet?"

"What for?"

"I have a feeling if he knew someone else had their hands on you there's a strong possibility that person wouldn't still be alive."

I sighed. "I can handle Jesse. The whole reason I called you was to ask about the knife. Did you get the picture I sent? Do you know what it is?"

"Based on the triangular shape, it looks like a lancet."

"A what?" I said.

"Scalpel."

"Like the kind you use to perform autopsies, right?"

"Similar. X-ACTO knives are sold everywhere. Except—"

"What?"

"The one in the picture you sent isn't the kind I see every day," she said. "It's unique."

"How so?"

"It's an obsidian scalpel with what appears to be a twelve millimeter blade from what I can tell by looking at the photo you sent me. Most surgeons use plain, ordinary, disposable scalpels, but this one would have probably been used several times."

"What's so special about it?"

"It's made from a type of volcanic glass. The cuts made with an obsidian are five hundred times sharper than your average steel scalpel."

"How is that beneficial in surgery?" I said.

"Incisions made with this type of blade heal faster. A surgeon might use it at the request of the patient. In most cases, it would be used whenever any fine cutting action is required."

"So I'm looking for someone in the medical profession then?"

"Anyone with medical training who'd have access to that sort of thing. People don't just walk around with these in their pockets."

Maddie took a deep breath. "Sloane, are you sure you're all right? Because I can take some time off. I know how hard it must be for you to be back in your hometown again. Say the word and I'm there."

"I'll be fine."

"You're not yourself, I can hear it in your voice. Look, I understand how it must feel to go back there after all this time, but stop running. Forget about the Sloane from the past and think about who you are now—tough, resilient, a fighter."

Out of the corner of my eye I spied a familiar flash of grey. "Damnit, I can't even get five minutes to myself."

"What's going on?" Maddie said.

"It's Jesse, he's coming."

CHAPTER 13

I slipped into the donut shop, slid across the red vinyl seat until I reached the corner of the booth and placed a call to Trista. Eight minutes later her burgundy minivan rolled into the parking lot. The windows were tinted the lightest shade of grey I'd ever seen on a vehicle, and on the back was a series of stickers of a stick family in white all lined up next to each other. I'd seen that type of thing on so many minivans over the years I'd begun to wonder if it was a free add-on with purchase. One look at Stick Doug gave me a renewed determination to find his killer.

I sent Jesse a quick text so he wouldn't put an APB out on me and promised we'd get together later that night for dinner like we'd planned the day before. I hoped to get some information out of him and not have to deal with him again. The more time we spent together, the more uncomfortable I felt. He was aggressive, just like he was when we were younger, but that wasn't all. He exerted a sort of confidence and determination I didn't remember him having before. And I didn't like it.

When I hopped into the van, Trista swept her sunglasses over her red, puffy eyes and looked at me. "Where to?"

Good question.

She pointed at the bakery. "Donuts sound good."

"No!"

It was only after I yelled that I realized the harsh way the word spewed out of my mouth. I placed my hand on her arm. "I'm sorry, I'm a little on edge. I'd like to get out of here if you don't mind. Anywhere else is fine, just get me out of the center of town."

Trista put the van in reverse and wheeled out of the parking lot. Several minutes later we stood in front of a black and white animal that she referred to as a 'paint.' The horse trotted forward in his stall and lowered his muzzle. Trista stroked him.

"This is Duke," she said. "Doug bought him a few years back."

"John Wayne fan?"

She nodded. "Doug owned every movie the man ever made."

"I've always wondered how John Wayne got his nickname," I said. "Figured it was given to him by another actor."

She shook her head. "A fireman named him that when he was a kid. He used to deliver papers with his dog named Duke. The fireman called them Big Duke and Little Duke."

"Wow. I had no idea."

"I didn't either until Doug gave me the backstory one night on John Wayne's life. I'm worried about him."

"The horse?"

She nodded. "He's barely eaten in days. It's like he senses something's wrong because Doug hasn't been here. He used to stop by after he got off work." Trista angled her head toward the next stall. "You ride?"

I backed up a few paces and waved my hands across each other. "I haven't ridden a horse since I was a kid."

"Why not?"

"I got bucked off once. Haven't had much of a desire to get back on one since."

Trista walked over to a pile of hay in the corner, sat down and indicated with her finger for me to sit next to her, but ever since we'd entered the barn I'd squeezed one of my hands over my nose to block the smell. She hadn't seemed to notice.

"Would you mind if we walked around outside instead?" I said.

She shrugged and followed me out of the stable. "I've been coming here every day since Doug died. I don't know why. I never paid much attention to his horse before, but now…"

"It makes you feel close to him, doesn't it?"

"In a way. In other ways I probably make it harder on myself by being here. I don't know why I do it. I guess I'm trying to hold on to him any way I can."

She stopped and leaned over a wooden fence post. I stood next to her. "Trista, I need to ask you a question."

She swirled some dirt around with the tip of her rounded boot and stared at the ground. "I know. Heather called me, and you're right…I should have told you. But he's dead, and I didn't want you to remember him that way. Besides," she shrugged, "he was only with her the one time."

I placed my hand on the fence post and watched the horses frolicking in the field next to where we stood. "You don't need to convince me—one night of infidelity doesn't change my feelings toward him. It was a mistake. He loved you. I don't doubt that."

Trista grimaced. "I wanted to beat the crap out of her, you know. Not for the cheating—I mean, I hated that part too, but I knew he could talk to her in a way he couldn't talk to me. I asked him a thousand times to open up and he still wouldn't."

"You understand why, right?"

She shook her head.

"He didn't want you to worry," I said. "Doug wanted you to see him for the man he wanted to be—if he spilled out all his problems to you, he would have felt like even more of a failure." I faced her. "So what. They slept together. The way I see it, Heather was more of a counselor to him than anything else. She was someone he confided in so he could get past his issues and back to his family."

She frowned. "He turned to her because he couldn't turn to me, you know. I got sick of asking and getting nowhere. So I became numb—to him, to the kids, everyone. I probably pushed him right into her."

"There's no shame for taking something to help you cope," I said.

A look of shock washed over Trista's face. Obviously Heather hadn't told her everything about our time together. She gave me a look like I just didn't get it. "What about when your doctor prescribes one pill a day but you take ten and you have to be rushed to the hospital to get your stomach pumped? What then?"

I put my arm around her shoulder. "There's nothing wrong with a wake-up call. We all need them from time to time. You're here, you're alive, and doing the best you can. You have three beautiful reasons to pick yourself up and move on. Your kids need you now more than ever."

CHAPTER 14

I was poised on a black velvet chair in an Italian restaurant. The décor was similar to most Italian restaurants I'd been in: Dangling vines of fake plastic grapes, bottles of red wine, and arched mirrors—lots of them. Jesse sat across from me. He shoveled a load of noodles into his mouth and didn't seem to mind the Alfredo sauce dripping down his chin. He retained his conversation without missing a beat. I clenched my fists under the table and resisted reaching for a napkin. He was a big boy, he could clean himself up.

"You don't know how many times I've thought about you over the years," he said. "Damn, it's good to see you, and you're lookin' fine tonight…wooh-eee!"

"Let's talk about Doug," I said.

"Always Doug with you. Man you're tight, Sloane. A hard ass, you know it? You gotta loosen up. It's like you've never been complimented before."

I'd been complimented plenty. The difference was

always in who was doing the complimenting and whether it was wanted or unwanted. Jesse either didn't know the difference or didn't care. I drew in a long breath. "Look, if you don't want to answer my questions, fine. I can leave."

I scooted my chair back, stood up and tossed my napkin in the center of the table.

Jesse waved a hand in the air. "Oh c'mon, Sloane. Sit back down, woman. I'll answer anything you want."

I stood there, unmoved, and considered my options, mostly for dramatic effect. When I thought it had reached its desired level, I lowered myself into the chair again.

"How much have you seen Doug over the years?" I said.

He leaned forward and rested his elbows on the table. "It's a small town. I'm a cop. I see everyone."

"Let me rephrase—how often have you spoken to him?"

"Pulled him over for drunk drivin' a couple months back. Guess that'd be the last time we were face to face."

"And?"

Jesse glared at me. "He was drunk, Sloane. I just said that."

"Did you arrest him?"

He shook his head.

"Why?"

He shrugged. "I don't know. Should have, I guess, but I didn't. I left his car there and gave him a lift home."

"That doesn't make sense to me," I said.

"Why—because I'm a police officer, my only option is to arrest him? I can't be an officer *and* a friend at the same time?"

"Arresting him is part of the job, right? Who knows what could have happened if you hadn't come along." I sighed. "Look, I cared for Doug too, but if he was driving drunk one night, he was probably doing it a lot more than you thought. Maybe locking him up for twenty-four hours would have taught him something."

Jesse frowned and gulped back some beer. "Nothing happened, and Doug's not even alive now, so who flippin' cares?"

"You don't need to do this, you know."

"What?"

"Keep things from me." I reached for my drink and took a sip. "Or maybe you do. You felt sorry for Doug that night, and it kept you from doing your job. The question is, why?"

"What does any of this have to do with why he's dead? He wasn't killed from a head-on collision."

My current line of questioning wasn't working. Next.

"Trista said they had a daughter in college."

Jesse's face tightened and he cleared his throat. "Alexa. Smart girl. Pretty little thing too."

"What can you tell me about her?"

"Uh, she's their daughter, she's in college. I'm a cop, not neighborhood watch. What more do you need to know?"

"Seems a little strange to me that Doug and Trista would throw away their scholarships to stick around here and raise a kid when they were still kids themselves."

Jesse spun his bottle round and round in circles on the tablecloth. "What did Trista tell you about Alexa?"

"Long story."

He winked. "I've got all night."

I shook my head. "No—she actually said it was a long story. That's all I got out of her."

"Have you spoken to Doug's parents?"

"Why would I—what do they have to do with it?"

"Rosalind might be able to shed some light on things for you."

"Doug's mother?"

He nodded. "She's your best bet. I don't know much. Seems to me you're goin' about this all wrong. You should focus on Doug. Why you're interested in Alexa is beyond me."

"So far you haven't been able to answer any of my questions," I said.

He just smiled and shoveled another spoonful of noodles into his mouth.

"If you can't help me, why are we here?" I said.

"I got you to go out with me. I'd say that's progress."

Jesse's words had become monotone, but it was obvious he was feeling me out, seeing what I knew while resisting my questions and not answering anything directly. He was hiding something from me, but what and why? I rolled my eyes. All this time—wasted. And I'd learned nothing. If it wouldn't have been for the incessant growl in my stomach, I would have left. But I stayed and we finished dinner and chitchatted about stupid things that had nothing to do with the reason I'd agreed to meet in the first place. My goal was to end the night without it being a total wash, so I tried one final topic.

"I ran into Heather Masterson the other day."

He raised an eyebrow. "Fun girl. We dated last year for a while."

"What happened?"

His nostril flared. "Other men happened. She started seeing Nate, and then out of nowhere she developed a thing for Doug."

"I heard—although, that's not how she described it."

He grabbed a napkin and wiped two hours of drool and sauce from his face. "Stalker should be that girl's middle name."

Finally, we were getting somewhere. I kept my mouth shut hoping I'd get more. And I did.

"She was his sponsor in AA."

"Yeah," I said, "I know."

"But you wanna know the best part? She wasn't an alcoholic."

I choked on the piece of ice I'd been twirling around in my mouth. "You're kidding, right?"

He shook his head. "She only pretended to have a problem so she could get closer to Doug. And she did."

"Sheesh, sounds like she attended the Candice school of naughty behavior."

Jesse laughed. "She probably did. They're friends."

"Candice lives here?" I said.

"No." He did air quotes with his fingers. "Beverly Hills."

"As in 90210?"

"As in an ailing eighty-something-year-old husband who's ready to kick the bucket and leave his millions to her. She's been around here a lot more lately and has taken Heather on as a kind of special needs project. At least that's how it seems to me."

"I walked down Candice memory lane on the cruise," I said. "And I have to say, I hadn't missed her."

He frowned. "Who would? She's already been with every guy in town, married and single. You wanna know the truth? I always thought she'd be dead by now. A jealous wife, a husband wanting to make sure she kept her mouth shut—it's crazy to me that Doug's dead while Candice lives to see another day."

Enough talk about Candice for the night. "So…where does Heather work, anyway?"

"She's a nurse at the hospital."

CHAPTER 15

"Let me give you a ride," Jesse said.

I managed a weak smile and tried to keep the I'm-ready-to-get-away-from-you look off my face. "I've already called a cab…so, I'll see you later?"

He pulled out his cell phone, dialed and cancelled the cab, just like that. "Looks like you don't need it anymore."

I'd played nice with Jesse since I arrived in town, but I wasn't sure how much longer I could manage being around him without becoming the cause of California's next major earthquake. But I didn't plan on seeing him again if I could help it, so what was another fifteen minutes?

Because of the recent events at the hotel and the sharp object found lodged in my door, the hotel staff was on edge and practically packed my bags for me. I decided I needed something a bit more private and splurged on some five-star digs that backed up against the entrance to Tehachapi

Mountain Park. And the best part was all the rooms were detached into free standing one-bedroom cabins—it was my best chance at privacy. All I needed now was to get there.

"So how's Nate?" I said. "He still lives here, I take it?"

Jesse made a left turn and nodded. "I see him every week at poker night." He glanced sideways at me. "I know what you're thinking, and you're wrong."

"What?"

"You said before you weren't sure it was a coincidence two friends in the same clique died within days of each other, but I'm telling you, it's the wrong direction to go in. The four of us all lead separate lives now; we have for years."

"You mean the two of you?" I said.

He frowned.

I continued. "I'm more interested in your lives back then, not the lives you lead now."

"Why?"

I shrugged. "I'm not sure yet—I feel like there's a connection between the past and the murders. I just need to find it."

We drove in silence for a time until I couldn't stand it anymore. "How *is* Nate?"

"Single."

"He never got married?"

Jesse laughed. "Yeah, to his cars...he owns Nate's Automotive in town."

"He always was a good salesman. I remember him talking Mrs. Webb into turning his F into an A in History class. I always thought he'd move away from here though."

"Didn't need to—why move when you have an established fan base?"

"True. When'd you see him last?"

"Couple nights ago. Poker was at his house this week."

"And where would that be?"

"Stallion Springs."

He looked over at me. "Nate is fine, Sloane. I'll call him if you want so you can put this theory of yours to rest."

I shook my head. "I'm sure you're right. I'll stop in and see him for myself."

Jesse pulled into the parking lot and the car lulled to a stop. I'd already prepared for immediate evacuation by securing my bag over my shoulder and wrapping my fingers through the latch. I tugged on it and the door swung open.

"Thanks for the ride," I said, hopping out, but before I could plant both feet on terra firma, Jesse grabbed my shirt and yanked me back. Apparently he had a plan of his own, and his blacked-out side windows gave him all the privacy he needed. My shirt ripped in two places, and in the few seconds I spent surveying the damage, Jesse had unbuckled his seatbelt and climbed on top of me.

"I want you," he groaned in my ear. "Say you want me too. Let's go back to your room and I'll show you how much I've thought of you over the years."

His hands forced their way inside my shirt, grappling my breasts. With one foot still out the door, I swung my body to the side, taking him with me. Our bodies fell onto the pavement next to the car. My hands collided with tiny pebbles of gravel, scraping my skin. I reached across, yanked back on his neck, and slapped him across the face.

He turned, enraged. "Really—again with the slapping?"

"Is this why you're a cop—so you can exert your power over women! Is that who you are now, Jesse?"

I scrambled to get off the ground and was met with resistance as he wrapped his arms around me, trying to hold me down. It was time to teach him a lesson from the Sloane book of what happened to a person who crossed the line.

"Sloane?" a voice shouted behind me.

I whipped my head around and stared up at a wide-eyed Giovanni sprinting in my direction. When he got within five feet, he took one look at my torn shirt and exposed bra and locked eyes with Jesse. Not good.

"What are you doing here?" I said.

But he didn't seem to hear me. His eyes were riveted on the palm of my left hand which was now bleeding. He hoisted Jesse into the air with a clenched hand to Jesse's neck and thrust him forward. Jesse's head smashed into the passenger-side window and it shattered, spilling pieces of glass all over the pavement.

In his shocked stupor, Jesse managed a weak, "I'm a cop—I'll have you arrested for assaulting a police officer."

It was a line I'd always remember as one of the stupidest comments to be uttered from a person's mouth. Jesse had no idea what it meant to cross Giovanni, but he was about to find out. For a cop in such good shape, I was surprised how easily Jesse was subdued. I bent over Giovanni and stared into Jesse's eyes.

Again he shouted, "I'll have him arrested, Sloane."

"No you won't, or I'll press charges for that little parlor trick you just pulled on me in the car."

He looked at Giovanni whose tight grip got even tighter. "I thought she wanted it, I swear."

I shook my head. "No you didn't."

I tugged on Giovanni's shoulder. "I just want him out of here. Preferably alive."

He eased up on the grip he had on Jesse and then tightened again. "Get in your car and leave—now," he said.

Jesse looked at me like he was waiting for me to speak as a witness for the defense.

"I don't know what to say," I said. "I feel like I don't know you anymore. I remember when I considered you a friend—but now…"

He averted his eyes and said nothing so I ended the conversation. "I never want to see you again, Jesse."

***

When we got inside the hotel room, Giovanni excused himself and made a call. I showered, and when I stepped out, he was back in the room hovering over a laptop sitting on a knotty pine desk.

I walked over and leaned over him. "Why are you here?"

He stared up at me and his eyes hardened. "Who was the man you were with tonight?"

"No one important. He's someone I used to know. I thought he might be able to give me some answers about what's been going on around here—I was wrong." I smiled. "Your turn."

He shrugged. "Madison thought you needed some company."

"Maddie called you one time and you decided to fly out here?"

He inserted his hand inside the tie that fastened my robe and pulled me close. "I missed you."

I closed my eyes for a moment and absorbed those

three little words. When I opened them again, he'd stood up, held out his hand and glanced toward the bedroom with all the passion of a kiss between two lovers that hadn't seen each other for years. My thoughts drifted away until nothing was left except his hand in mine and a bed that never looked so inviting.

CHAPTER 16

The view from my new hotel room offered a significant upgrade from my previous three-and-a-half star digs. The landscape outside was breathtaking. I paused a moment and took it in. Fall had always been my favorite time of year. Leaves shook with confidence inviting the world to view their magnificent color-changing act. It was their last hurrah before they expired, fluttered to the ground and were swept away and crushed by a cold, unforgiving wind. I watched one such leaf detach from a branch and get whisked away until I couldn't see it any longer. It reminded me of my own life and how I'd drifted away, abandoning my roots. I'd never even stopped and looked back. Until now.

Giovanni caressed my shoulders from behind. "You're freezing," he said. "I'll make you something hot to warm you up."

I spun around. "You didn't need to come out here, you know. I mean, I'm glad you did. But if you're worried about me, I'm fine, no matter what Maddie says."

He glanced out the window. "This town—it's where you grew up?"

I nodded.

"When was the last time you were here?"

"Several years, but even then, I was only here for the day. Once I graduated high school, I left this place and never had the urge to come back."

"And how do you feel now that you've returned?"

I sighed. "Have you ever felt everyone around you was keeping a secret or multiple secrets and you were the only one who wasn't in on it?"

The look on his face indicated he didn't understand where I was coming from. "No one has ever been any good at keeping secrets from me."

I was afraid to ask why or what measures he took to convince people to reveal the most private parts of their lives.

"There's something going on around here," I said. "Something big. I just need to figure out what."

He tapped my nose with his finger. "You will, I'm sure of it."

I shook my head. "You have so much confidence in me."

"And yet I know so little about your life before I came to be a part of it."

I felt the same way about him. Both of us wanted to

be honest and open with each other, but when it came to a life confessional, we both held back.

He continued. "We're here, in the town where you spent your childhood, and yet, in the time I've known you, you've never talked about this place. I'm a patient man, Sloane. I've never pushed or asked anything from you I didn't think you were ready to give. But I want to know everything about you. Don't be afraid to let me in."

No one had ever managed that level of closeness with me, and I wondered if he'd agree to the same. I'd always been good at giving small pieces of my life as long as I didn't have to release every little facet. I'd offer up a snack here and there, but never a full-course meal. Standing in front of me was the first guy to ever make me burn with the desire to break free from the shackled locks I'd placed on myself. I didn't want to live like that anymore—it wasn't fair. Not to me, not to him.

I brushed by Giovanni, grabbed my bag and shot him a wink. "Let's go for a drive."

***

I wound Giovanni's rented Ferrari 599 GTB through the various back roads of Bear Valley Springs until I came to the sign I was looking for: Black Forest Drive. It amazed me how

I could be away for so long but still cruise the streets without the need to jog my memory. The scenery had changed, but it was like no time had passed at all.

At the end of the cul-de-sac was a cement driveway leading to a two-story home tucked between a myriad of pine trees that surrounded the house on all sides. The stone exterior was in disrepair, but intact. Not a single piece of rock had dislodged.

I parked the car, got out and turned to Giovanni. "This is where I grew up."

"It's…"

"Small and rundown, I know."

He smiled. "I was going to say charming."

I turned away from him and stared back at the house. It was vacant and had been for some time, but looking through the framed window in front was like a doorway into the past.

Two people stood in the center of the living room, arguing—a man and a woman. The man yelled, no, screamed something at the woman. "What did you say to me?" he said. And then he raised his hand. She knew what it meant and tried to back away. But she wasn't fast enough. His hand flew through the air, the backside catching the woman's cheek. She yelped in pain. Her hand rushed to the inflamed area, and she rubbed it up and down until the man snatched it away. "Don't be a sissy, take what's coming to you," he shouted, and he hit her again—this time, harder.

A soft voice from the back of the house squeaked out, "No!" The man squinted and glared down the hallway, but saw nothing. He could have let it go, pretended he didn't hear it, but he wasn't in the business of learning lessons—he was in the business of teaching them. He whipped his belt through the loops of his pants, folded it in half and snapped it for dramatic effect. The sound echoed through the house. The woman screamed, "Don't touch them! Don't hurt my babies!" The man answered by striking her on the back with the belt. She crumbled to the floor, and in a last ditch effort to stop him, she reached out, grabbing his ankle with her hand. He shrugged it off, smashed his boot into it and then stepped over her and proceeded down the hallway.

I wanted to shout out to the little girl: Run and hide Gabby, run and hide, hurry! But, she stood there, frozen, like her feet were welded to the floor. When the man reached her he cracked the belt over her head like he was whipping a horse. Tears streamed down her cheeks and she held her hand out as a shield to protect her. "No, Daddy! Stop!" He looked at her, his face filled with rage. "You want me to stop? You're telling me what to do now—is that it? You girls are all the same, just like your bitch of a mother." And then he brought the belt down on her again.

Out of the shadows another girl appeared, a wooden

baseball bat gripped in her tiny hand. The man was taller than she was by at least two feet, but he was too busy stooped over the other girl to feel the thick weight of the wood when it embraced the back of his head. The man went down, and the girl with the bat dropped it on the ground and reached her hand out to her sister. "Come with me, Gabby. I'll protect you." The two girls ran hand-in-hand through the living room until they reached their mother. She shooed them out the door with her hand. "Sloane," the woman said, "get your sister out of here—go to the neighbor. Call the police. Hurry!"

I blinked my eyes a few times and was back in the front yard staring into the window of the house, but this time, the images in my head were gone, and the room was empty.

"My mom said she was leaving," I said, "and taking us with her. But then he saw the bags on the edge of the bed. They were packed. Hers and ours, but not his. It was the first time she'd ever stood up to him."

Giovanni had a puzzled look on his face. "Are you all right?"

I shook my head back and forth, aware of the revelation I'd given. "Reliving an old memory from my childhood," I said. "It's nothing. I shouldn't have come here."

He took my hands in his. "It's okay to face your fears. They make you strong."

I shrugged. "I hate to admit it, but being here makes me feel weaker than I have in a long time. I don't know what I was thinking—that maybe if I faced it after all these years I'd somehow feel empowered. But, I don't. I just want to run and never stop."

"What the lion cannot manage to do, the fox can."

I squinted my eyes at him.

He smiled down at me. "German proverb."

"I'm not sure I grasp its meaning," I said.

"You are stronger than you realize."

We got back into the car, but this time, Giovanni drove.

"I haven't been back to my house since I was eighteen," I said.

"Why today?"

I leaned back into the warmth of the heated leather seat. "Sometimes I feel like I can face my demons now because I'm older, wiser, healthier. But the truth is, it's probably better to stay away than to force myself to relive a nightmare I've tried so hard to forget."

He smiled like he understood. "Is that what the house represents to you?"

"I felt like I was twelve years old again. I felt trapped and like it was up to me to save my sister and my mom from my…my monster of a father."

"Then you don't ever need to return to the house again.

Closure comes in many different ways."

"Believe me," I said, "I'd strike a match and burn the house to the ground if I could, and I'd watch until every last sliver of wood was gone forever. It's been vacant for years. My mother left the house to me in her will, but I couldn't ever bring myself to move anyone into it. It's like I thought they would feel the negative energy and it would ruin their lives just like it ruined mine—like a stupid house is to blame for my father's actions."

"Back there you said your mother tried to leave. What happened?"

"My grandfather happened, and my dad never saw us again."

"Why didn't he get you out of there sooner?"

"I wondered that for years, but when I was old enough my grandmother told me he didn't know. She wouldn't say who told him, but it wasn't my mother. She always knew how much her father hated my dad, so she kept things from him."

"Is he still alive—your father?"

I nodded. "He's in a rest home in Bakersfield. I'd be surprised if he ever gets any visitors."

Giovanni gripped the steering wheel a bit tighter with his hand. "As it should be."

"I read an article in a magazine once that I've never been

able to forget."

He raised a brow. "What did it say?"

"Girls grow up to marry men just like their fathers. And I did."

"Would you say I'm like him?"

I pondered the possibility in my mind. There was more than a fair to midland chance in Giovanni's line of work that he gave the order to make someone pay, and not in cash. But I couldn't imagine him laying a hand on me or any woman for that matter. I shook my head. "No, you're not like him at all. But you do remind me of my grandfather."

CHAPTER 17

The next morning Giovanni left me to tend to some business he had in L.A. for a couple days which was fine—I got more done on my own. It was a shock he'd shown up in the first place, but a pleasant one, and I was starting to get used to his affinity for surprises.

I turned my attention to the grey building towering over me. Heather Masterson exited through the revolving door a little after one pm. I was leaning up against her car, waiting.

She jumped an inch or two when she saw me. "What are you doing here?"

"I came to see you."

"About what?"

"Both Doug and Rusty were stabbed with a knife, and you work at a hospital. Something you failed to mention when we were together before."

She shrugged. "It shouldn't matter what I do—I'd never hurt Doug, and I barely knew Rusty."

I whipped out my cell phone, found the photo I'd taken of the scalpel and shoved my phone in front of her face. "Ever seen one of these?"

She shook her head. "I don't use that kind. Mine are disposable. Why all the questions?"

"Why'd you go to AA if you weren't really a drunk?"

She scrutinized the parking lot, looking in all directions and then lowered her voice to a whisper. "You can't say things like that out here—at my workplace."

"What—Alcoholics Anonymous?" I said with a raised voice. "Why? You're not an alcoholic, so it shouldn't offend you."

She tapped her white plastic Crocs shoe on the ground. "Who is filling your head with all these lies?"

"You told me you became Doug's sponsor because he asked you."

"I wasn't lying—he did."

"I'm curious," I said, "did he ask you because you pretended to be someone you're not? And while we're on the subject of questions, here's another one. How many lies did you have to tell Doug before he was weak enough to hop in bed with you?"

Her face flushed, first a reddish color and then a pale white. She darted over to the passenger door of her car and got in. I opened the driver's side and sat down.

"What are you doing? This is *my* car—get out!"

"Where to?" I said.

"Excuse me?"

I smiled. "This can work one of two ways—one, I stay in the car and we drive around together until I get some answers. Or two, I get in my car and follow you around until I'm satisfied you're not the person I'm after. It could take days, weeks…"

She gulped a swig of something that looked like water in a clear plastic container she held in her hand and shouted, "Okay!"

I leaned back and crossed my arms.

"I met Doug when I went to open an account at the bank last year. I remembered him from high school, but hadn't seen him around much since then. Every time I went in to make a deposit or something, he was so nice to me."

"Wasn't that part of his job?"

She shrugged. "I guess so, but there was something about him that drew me in. He seemed so perfect. And happy. It wasn't until I followed…"

"You mean stalked him?"

She shook her head. "It wasn't like that, I swear. After work, he wouldn't go home. He went to the bar. It didn't take long for me to realize he had a drinking problem. And then one night I overheard a guy at the bar tell him about AA.

Doug said he would start going."

"So you joined?"

She nodded.

"And you didn't feel bad about being around all those people who were trying to get help for their real problems?" I said.

"I thought I was doing him a favor."

"He had a wife for that—and a family," I said. "It wasn't your place to interfere."

"Trista was popping pills, how the hell was that helping!"

"You don't have any idea what Trista's life has been like living with an alcoholic for so many years—don't judge her."

Heather smirked. "What, she's your friend now so you have to stick up for her?"

"There it is," I said.

"What?"

"Candice rears her ugly head at last."

"Candice and I are friends, so what?"

"The more you talk, the more you sound just like her," I said. "Don't let her fool you—she has a bad reputation around here."

"Had."

I laughed. "You don't think she lost the title because she moved do you?"

She crossed one leg over the other and glared at me,

and I wasn't sure whether it was because I'd slammed her friend or knew her secrets or both.

"Did Candice push you to make a move on Doug?" I said.

"It was more of a challenge. She told me I couldn't, and I knew I could. And I did."

It was one of those moments where you looked at a person but no longer saw the same thing you did the first time. Heather's exterior facade vanished, and I was left with a grueling image of what kind of person she was beneath her hardened exterior. It disgusted me.

I opened the door to her car, got out and closed it behind me. She crossed over to the driver's side and pressed the button to lower the window.

Exasperated, she said, "Wait—where are you going? Are you going to follow me?"

I didn't look back.

CHAPTER 18

After spending time with Heather, I wasn't sure she had what it took to butcher someone. On the whole, she was a snake of a person, but more of a gopher than a viper where murder was concerned. Candice, on the other hand, was another story. One I'd deal with later. At the moment I had a much older woman I needed to reacquaint myself with in Stallion Springs.

A text popped up on my phone from Trista saying dinner had been moved to tonight. Alexa had come home a day early as a surprise. I glanced at the time on the dash; I still had a good four hours before I needed to be there, and I wanted to make the most of it.

I stopped at the local gas station before heading out and wasn't surprised when I looked over and spotted Jesse in his patrol vehicle next to me. The only difference was, when I got out to pump the gas, he didn't even look in my direction, not even a glance, and I refused to believe he hadn't seen me.

His Sloane radar was state of the art.

He shifted his head around and looked at something in front of me, but I couldn't look away. My eyes were riveted on his face. His red, bruised, swollen face. I tapped on his window but he jerked his head in the opposite direction.

"Jesse, I know you can see me," I said. "What happened to your face?"

He let the window down a crack. "Go away, Sloane. You said you never wanted to see me again, so why are you talking to me?"

The area below his eye was puffy, like he'd been skewered by the horn of a bull and let it sit for a while. I reached my hand through the opening, turned his face toward me, and gasped. "Who did this to you?"

He shook his head. "Oh, that's good…real good."

"What?"

"Like you don't know."

"What's that supposed to mean?"

He leaned back and squinted his left eyelid at me. The other eyelid didn't look like it was capable of moving. "You really don't know, do you? I tell you what, why don't you call your boyfriend and ask him what happened after you went inside the hotel last night?"

I shrugged. "It wasn't Giovanni—he was with me all night."

"I never said he was the one who did this to me."

"Then you're implying he knows who did."

He grabbed my hand, shoving it out the window in one powerful thrust and then slammed his car into gear and peeled out.

***

Thirty minutes later I arrived at the estate of Rosalind Ward, Doug's mother. She was known as the woman in town who had her hands in everything from city ordinances to simple street names—Tehachapi had both a Rosalind Drive *and* a Ward Avenue. Rosalind also took pride in the fact that she owned the property next door to the late Jack Palance, an actor I'd once served dinner to when I was a clumsy no-name waitress in high school.

The moment I drove up the long, windy road I felt her eyes glaring down at me from her second-story window, much like an eagle sizing up its prey. As the sparrow in the situation, I exited my car and approached the front door with caution, but before I had the chance to crunch up my hand and knock, she'd opened the door and looked over every last inch of me. I obliged her by doing the same. She wore a white rayon shirt with a white cami underneath and white polyester slacks. Her short hair was curled to perfection in a short coif like Elizabeth Taylor wore in 1952. Every lock was in place, and her skin, albeit milky and smooth, looked as though it had gone through a facelift or two. Maybe even three, she certainly had the money. No woman her age looked that good naturally, did they?

Rosalind tapped her fingers on the glass panel of the door. "I don't like surprises. There's a reason God invented the telephone."

"Huh," I said. "I always thought it was Alexander Graham Bell."

She wasn't amused.

I stuck my hand out. "You probably don't remember me. My name is Sloane Monroe. I was a friend of Doug's."

She shook my hand like she was afraid I'd transfer some of my germs onto her and then folded one arm over the other. "I wish people would stop coming out here. I get it. Everyone feels bad. Everyone wants us to know about the time he pulled to the side of the road to help them fix a flat tire or when he held the door open for some old lady with a bag of groceries in her hands. It's like no one gets it. He was my son. I raised him. Of course he was all those things."

I slid my hands in my pockets and met her gaze. "I was on the boat when he was killed."

"Good for you."

It occurred to me now wasn't the best time to let her

know I was overseeing my own investigation. "As a friend, I'm just trying to sort out what happened."

She gave me a sideways glance. "That won't be necessary. We are working with the authorities to recover his body. It's handled. Is that all?"

I stood there, unsure of what to say next.

She squinched her beady eyes at me. "You don't remember me, do you?"

"Sure I do—everyone knows who your family is in this town."

She smiled, pleased with my comment of flattery. "And I'm familiar with yours."

Of course she was—who was I to think time would make everyone forget a father who made the front page of the town paper for all the wrong reasons.

She gave her comment ample time to sink in and then continued. "I'm the one who alerted your grandfather about your ahh, situation with your father. Your grandfather was good friends with my own father, you know, before he retired and ran off to Park City. I figured it was the least I could do to help your poor mother out. It was obvious she wasn't going to do anything seeing how she didn't want anyone to know what was really going on, but when I saw you and your sister running up the street that day, I knew my tongue had been stilled long enough. I wasn't placed on this Earth to stand idly by like some kind of ninny."

I wanted to speak, but couldn't find the words. Why couldn't I remember seeing her that day?

She frowned. "Well, I suppose if I was in your shoes, I would have blocked my childhood out too."

I wanted to shrink down until I was small enough to fit inside my handbag.

She cocked her head to the side and curled her lips into a snarly smile like we were playing war of the words with each other and she'd just won. "Why else did you come here, Sloane?"

Manipulation 101 at its finest. I forced myself out of her head and back into mine. "Why didn't Doug go to college?"

She shrugged. "It wasn't the path he was meant to take in life."

"But he had a scholarship—I'm curious about why he gave it up to get married. Couldn't he have completed school and then married? Wasn't that what you wanted for him?"

She looked over her left shoulder for a moment like she wanted to be sure whoever was inside the house couldn't hear and then she stepped out onto the porch and slid the door closed behind her.

"What did Trista tell you?"

"It's more of what she didn't tell me that I'm interested in," I said.

"Such as?"

"Why'd Doug have a drinking problem?"

"Excuse me?"

"I know he was in AA."

She turned her palms up like 'so what' and said, "Lots of people go there."

"So you weren't aware how big his problem was or how many years he'd been like that?"

She averted her eyes and gazed out at an empty field overrun with wild poppies and sagebrush. "I'm not comfortable with your questions."

It was nice to turn the tables for a change.

"Something drove him to drink, Mrs. Ward, and I don't believe it has anything to do with Trista."

She thrust her hand over her chest. "I never said it did."

"What happened while he was in high school? There was an event, something that caused Doug to give up his football scholarship, what was it?"

I stood back and waited to see if she had the courage to mention Alexa. From the way her lips tightened into a circular ball, I'd hit on something big. She braced her body against the door and stood like a statue for several seconds, and then folded one hand over the other and tried to act like I was a neighbor who came over to bum a cup of sugar.

"I'd like you to go now," she said. "All your questions

have made me tired."

I glanced down at my phone and noticed the time. "That's all right," I said. "I'm late for dinner with Trista anyway."

She lifted a brow at me. "Oh?"

"Trista invited me over to meet Alexa—I guess she's home from college for the weekend."

The look on her face before I turned to walk toward my car was something I never thought a woman such as Rosalind Ward was capable of. Fear.

CHAPTER 19

Since I was already in the area and still had three hours to kill, I thought I'd take a moment to visit my old friend Nate before going to Trista's house for dinner. Of the Rat Pack bunch, we had been the closest. My junior year we'd even attended the Sadie Hawkins dance together. My mom never had much money once she became a single parent, and since it was up to the girl to spring for matching shirts for the event, the most I'd been able to provide at the time was a pair of red sweaters on blue light special at the Kmart in Mojave. The best thing about Nate was he didn't care. He wore it with a pair of acid-washed jeans and Ray-Ban Wayfarer sunglasses and practically started a new trend. It could have been a shirt made of cellophane wrap—it didn't matter. If Nate wore it, everyone assumed it was cool, and the next week at school, a new fad was born, all thanks to The Natemeister.

    Nate lived on a ranch passed down to him by his

parents when they retired and left to travel the world in their Winnebago. Of course, once they moved out, he bulldozed the ranch-style home and replaced it with a shiny new bachelor pad that towered over all the other homes in the valley. He was a lot of flash and flare all balled up into one giant kid who refused to grow up and face adulthood.

The gate to the ranch was open when I arrived, but I still took a moment to admire the oversized letter N welded into the center. A shiny silver BMW sat in the driveway with a dealer plate attached to the back window. I parked beside it, and when I walked by, I noticed the driver's side of the car was dented in like it had been in a recent collision. Interesting. Since he had the top down, I poked my head in and wasn't surprised to discover a pair of black Ray-Ban Wayfarer sunglasses on the dash. Some things never changed.

I ascended the twenty-something steps to the second-story front entrance and rang the doorbell. No answer. I jiggled the handle. Locked. I walked back down the stairs and around the side of the house and spied a sliding glass door leading to the backyard. It was open. I peered in and saw no one, but what my eyes couldn't make out, my nose made up for in the form of an overwhelming stench that smelled like a slaughtered cow.

I cupped my hand over my mouth, squeezed my nose

with the other and yelled out, "Nate? You here?"

Silence.

I stepped inside, and as I neared the kitchen, I located the cause of the odor. Several packages of hamburger had been left out on the counter like he was preparing for a party, except it looked like they'd sat there for days. They were brown, and dried blood had seeped out and was fused to both the packages and the countertop. Wherever Nate was, it couldn't have been anywhere near a smell like that.

I started to head out the door when something barked. In the doorway down the hall, a cute little pug dog appeared. It looked at me, turned around and vanished. I followed. When I reached the room the dog was in I was overtaken once again by an odor far worse than anything I'd ever smelled in my life. I leaned my head inside the room and let out a scream that rivaled Jamie Lee Curtis in *Halloween*. Flattened on the master bed was the decomposing body of a man I wished was anyone other than Nate. A knife protruded from his chest. I took one baby step closer which proved to be a big mistake and then whipped my body around, fled outside and vomited into the hedges.

After it seemed everything was out of my system, I dialed 9-1-1. The operator answered and I said, "There's been a homicide."

I gave her the information and she gave me her usual

spiel about how she wanted me to stay on the phone, but I'd done what I needed to, and I wasn't going anywhere until police got there. I hung up and dialed again.

"I know, I know. You're mad at me for sending him down there," a voice said on the other end. "But before you say anything, you need to understand, I thought it was in your best interest."

"Maddie, I'm at a…there's a dead body, and…"

"Whoa, whoa, whoa. Slow down. You're with a dead body? Did you kill someone?"

"No. I stopped by to see an old friend and I think he's the dead guy. I mean, from the five seconds I was in there I could tell the body had started to decompose, and I haven't seen him in a long time, but who else could it be? Once a detective gets here—assuming the town has a homicide unit—I'm sure I won't be able to find out anything, so I was hoping you could…"

"How long has the guy been dead do you think?"

"I don't know," I said.

"All right, you've seen the body up close, right?"

"Yeah…"

"Describe it to me. What did it look like?"

"Bloated," I said. "Kind of a greenish color."

"Does his skin look like marble?"

I thought about it for a moment, and actually, it did.

"Yeah."

"Have you upchucked yet?"

"Multiple times."

"All right, then I need you to go back into the house and send me some photos of the body—get as close as you can, okay?"

"I don't think my stomach can handle round two," I said.

"You can do this," she said. "Get to the bathroom as quick as you can. Open the medicine cabinet if he has one or whatever he keeps stuff like that in and look for some Vicks VapoRub. Stick a good chunk of it under your nose. I mean a big one—plop it on there. It'll help with the smell. Then go back into the bedroom, snap whatever photos you can and send them to me."

CHAPTER 20

I returned to the hotel, discarded the clothes I'd worn that day outside in the dumpster and showered for what felt like several hours. But it didn't matter. The smell was in my nostrils and clung to my body like a wet bikini. No matter how much soap I used, I couldn't get the stench of rotting flesh to go away—not completely.

After my shower, I slumped down on the bed and allowed the past few hours to settle in around me. I wished I could have stomached Nate's house long enough to get a good look at everything, but that chance came and went when the wheels of the first police car squealed to a stop in Nate's front yard followed by another vehicle that contained the police chief and one of his sergeants. It was my cue to leave. The few photos I took I forwarded to Maddie. But since they were all surface shots, she could only estimate his death which she agreed could have occurred on poker night. The question was: Why hadn't anyone discovered him until now?

I regained all five senses, got dressed and texted Trista. I had one final stop to make before heading over for dinner: Nate's Automotive. When I arrived, I fully expected my car to be swarmed with salesman like a bunch of peppy cheerleaders at a car wash, but when the wheels touched the inside perimeter of the lot, nothing happened. I parked and searched for signs of life, but the area was more deserted than the town of Tombstone in the thirties.

I entered the dealership and looked around until I spotted a warm body. A boy with long black cornrows and a slender frame weighing in at about a buck fifty, approached me.

"Hey," he said. "What can we do for you today?"

"Why isn't anyone out on the lot?"

He laughed. "You've never been here before, have you?"

I shook my head. "Why?"

"We don't do that here."

"What?"

"Pester customers. We let you to come to us. No pressure. It's better that way."

"Nate teach you that?"

He nodded. "Do you know him?"

"We went to school together."

From his chipper attitude I deduced he hadn't heard the news about Nate's untimely demise, but it hadn't been long since I'd made the discovery.

"When was the last time you saw Nate?" I said.

"He's in Fiji, and he doesn't take kindly to phone calls when he's on vacation unless it's an emergency."

It explained why his body went unnoticed for days.

"How long has he been gone?"

He shrugged. "A few days I guess."

It added to my suspicion that the last time anyone saw him alive was poker night. I swallowed and realized if I wanted to get the details on Nate's final hours, I'd have to talk to Jesse—yet again.

"Did Nate vacation alone?"

He swiped his hand through the air like he was swatting a fly. "Naw, he took someone with him."

"Do you know who?" I said.

Cornrow Boy yelled over his shoulder to another guy who stood several feet away. "Hey, you know the name of the girl Nate took to Fiji?"

The other boy scratched his head. "Ahhh, I think her name was Janice?"

Cornrow Boy shook his head. "Naw man, that's not right. It started with a C." He slapped the thigh of his pants with his hand and laughed. "I actually heard Nate call her Candy once, cuz she smelled so sweet, but Candy wasn't her real name or nothin'."

It couldn't have been. Could it?

"Was her name Candice?" I said.

In unison both boys nodded. "Yeah, that's right."

The other guy winked at Cornrow Boy. "For an older woman, she is F-I-N-E fine, mmm mmmh!"

"How long had Nate been dating Candice?"

Cornrow Boy threw his head back and thundered with laughter. "You may have known Nate back in the day, but you obviously don't know nothin' about him now. Nate's never *with* anyone. He dates two, three girls at a time."

The two boys glanced at each other and nodded like they wanted to smack hands together in a high five.

"Did the girls Nate dated know he was with more than one woman at the same time?"

Cornrow Boy looked at me. "Uh, I dunno. That Candice chick didn't."

"How do you know?" I said.

"Cuz she found out he was dating some other girl and drove her car into his brand new beamer—get this— while my man was driving it."

The other guy nodded. "That chick's got balls, yo."

"And he still wanted to take Candice on vacation?"

By this time the other kid had walked over and was eager to join the conversation. "Nate likes the feisty ones."

"Yeah," Cornrow Boy said. "The crazier the better."

CHAPTER 21

It made me uncomfortable to be even a minute late for any event no matter how simple, but when I arrived at Trista's house carrying a pie in each hand from one of the local bakeries, no one seemed to mind my tardiness. One look at Trista's smiling face revealed she hadn't heard the news about Nate either. And with all three kids around, it wasn't the right time to tell her.

"C'mon in. I was just showing Alexa a picture of us from senior year," she said.

"I don't remember us ever being in a picture together."

We walked into the living room. A plastic bin the size of a shoebox rested on the coffee table. It was filled with photos of Trista at different stages in her life. She shuffled through a few of them and said, "Ah, here it is," and then handed it to me.

The photo had been taken on the homecoming float in 1991. The two of us were arm in arm in our black, white, and green Warrior paint that covered both our faces. The paint masked a lot, but couldn't hide my bright blue eye shadow or my spiral-permed hair.

Trista pointed at the photo. "I put that spirit paint on your face. Do you remember now?"

I didn't, but it was one of those situations where I rationalized how much better a white lie was than hurting her feelings.

"Good times," I said.

A girl with blond crimped hair stepped into the kitchen. She looked over at me and said, "Hey."

Trista held her hand out like she was giving a formal presentation. "This is my daughter, Alexa."

"I hear you want to be a doctor," I said.

Her cheeks flushed and she teetered back on the heels of her Mary Jane shoes. "Yeah, one day."

"I'll go check on dinner," Trista said.

I glanced at Alexa. "Are you an intern?"

She nodded. "I work a couple hours here and there at Guardian."

"Never heard of it," I said.

"It's a children's hospital."

"Is that what you want to go into—pediatrics?"

She nodded. "I love working with kids."

Trista emerged from the kitchen donning hot pads on

both hands and carrying several pieces of silverware. "Who's ready for dinner?"

***

Dinner came and went, and while Trista whisked the twins off to bed, I sat on the sofa with Alexa. She smoothed her hand over the cloth couch cushion and glanced in my direction several times but didn't say anything.

"Is there something you want to ask me?" I said.

She shrugged. "I don't know."

"Because if you do, it's okay. You can ask me anything you like."

She bit the corner of her lip. "Do you umm…think you'll find the person who hurt my dad?"

I tilted my head and leaned closer. "Did your mom tell you what happened?"

"She said my dad was in a fight with someone and he fell overboard. My brothers think it was an accident, but I know better, and I heard the neighbors say you were some kind of a detective. Are you?"

I nodded.

Her eyes widened. "Then you'll find who did it, right?"

"I hope so," I said. "How are you doing with all this?"

"It's weird, I guess. I'm sad he's gone, but it wasn't like I was his favorite."

"What do you mean?"

Alexa rose, walked to the pantry, took out a bag of cookies and plopped back down on the sofa. She tugged at the bag with her hands, and when it didn't open at the seam, she tossed it on the coffee table in front of her, bent over and rested her face in her hands. "I know my dad loved me, but he loved my brothers more."

I snatched the cookie bag, opened it, and slid it next to her. "I'm sure that's not true. What makes you think that?"

She raised her head up and wiped her moistened eyes on the sleeve of her shirt. "I dunno. I can't explain it. I mean, I know he loved me. I was his kid, so he had to, but the way he looked at me was different. When my brothers were born I felt like I didn't fit in."

It was hard for me to believe Doug would ever shun one of his own children, and yet, she seemed certain about his feelings for her. I thought about my own insecurities as a child and my feelings of abandonment from a father whose only favorite was himself and a bottle he called Jack D.

Alexa removed her hands from her face and looked at me. "I keep thinking I should come home so I can be here for my mom. It's not like it would be forever. I can go back to college next semester."

"Your mom is so proud of what you've accomplished

already. I'm sure she'd want you to stay in school."

She shrugged. "Maybe."

"Does your mom know how you feel?"

"Yeah. She said she wouldn't allow it, but I think she would. She can't force—"

Trista entered the room with plates of pie in each hand and glanced at Alexa. "Can't force you to do what?"

Alexa stood up. "Nothing, I'm going to my room."

Once she was out of sight, Trista handed me a slice of pie and sat the other's down. "What was that all about?"

"Nothing, really."

Trista rubbed her hands together. "Alexa hasn't talked much since she got here. I have no idea what she's going through—and I'm probably not doing a good job of being there for her right now—I can't even take care of myself."

"You remember what it was like at her age," I said. "Alexa is processing a lot of her emotions internally. I'm sure she'll talk to you when she's ready."

I knew precious little about the world of teenagers except what it felt like when I was one, but it seemed like sound advice.

Trista grabbed a plate of pie, scooped up a piece on a fork and took a bite. "Have you found out anything new since I last saw you?"

The time had come for me to make a decision about

whether it would be better for her to hear about Nate from me or from everyone else in town.

"Did Doug and Nate ever spend any time together?" I said.

Trista blinked a few times. "Nate Vargas?"

I nodded.

"We bought our cars from him."

"Yeah," I said, "but, did Doug ever see him for anything other than business?"

"Uh, no. Nate's lifestyle is umm—how can I put this—a lot different than ours. We were all about family, and he was, well, about being eighteen years old forever. Why?"

There wasn't an easy way to say it, so I grabbed her hand and blurted it out.

"I hate to be the one to tell you this, but I think it would be better coming from me."

A look of concern spread across her face. "What's happened?"

"I went to Nate's house earlier today."

"So you saw him?"

"Yeah, except when I found him, it wasn't what I expected."

She rolled her eyes. "Was he with a woman? Wouldn't surprise me. He's been with about every girl in town."

"He wasn't with anyone," I said. "He was dead."

CHAPTER 22

After a few hours of Trista going from very frazzled to a little less frazzled, she took something to help her sleep. I waited for it to kick in and then stopped by Alexa's room and let her know her mom was having a rough night. Alexa promised she would stay with her. I waited for things to quiet down and then took my leave.

When I returned to my own home-away-from-home I sent a text to Jesse.

> WE NEED TO TALK ABOUT POKER NIGHT.
> YOU MAY HAVE BEEN THE LAST ONE TO SEE NATE ALIVE.
> I KNOW WHAT I SAID, BUT CALL ME—PLEASE.

Then I called Giovanni.

"I was just thinking of you luce mia," he said.

The phrase *luce mia* was one among many phrases he used that I didn't understand. He said it often, and after I'd heard it several times and guessed it meant everything from me being loose—which couldn't have been his intention—to my love or my lover, I gave in and googled. Its meaning: *My light*.

"Did you attack Jesse?" I said.

"Is that what he told you?"

"His face said it more than anything."

Giovanni's voice never wavered. "I was with you all night."

"After you made a phone call outside the room first."

He sighed. "I made one business call, yes."

"And did it have anything to do with Jesse?"

A brief pause and then, "It did."

"So where is he?" I said.

"Who?"

"Your sidekick, bodyguard, whatever you call him—Lucio."

"Around."

Around in Giovanni speak meant he'd left Lucio at the hotel to keep an eye on me while he was away. Giovanni respected my independence and never stood in the way of my investigations, but he also looked out for my safety. He both respected and protected me at the same time. It was something I hadn't gotten used to yet.

"And did he—"

"Give Jesse a reminder about how not to treat women?" Giovanni said. "He did."

If there was one thing I appreciated, it was his honesty.

"I believe his face got the message," I said. "Can you tell Lucio to back off?"

"If your police friend doesn't touch you again, that can be managed."

We talked for a while longer about things that didn't have to do with Jesse, the town, or the murders, and then ended the call. It was strange. Although we'd known each other a short time, when he wasn't around, I missed him. It didn't matter whether I hadn't seen him for five minutes or five hours. I found myself thinking of when we'd be together again. It was a feeling I hadn't felt for any other man before.

I grabbed a blanket, reclined on the loveseat and went over what I knew about the case so far. Doug had been stabbed by, I assumed, the same person who killed Rusty and Nate. To an outsider, it probably looked like the work of a serial killer who could even be tied to some random cases in neighboring counties. Doug had been stabbed multiple times, which led me to believe one thing: He was the practice round. With Rusty and Nate, the killer was more methodical and precise, managing to deliver death by a single stab wound to the chest and then the knife was left as a representation of their crime, as if to say *look at me, look what I did.*

The knife in Nate's chest was long and thin, unlike the short, thick blade used on Rusty. Had the killer hand selected specific knives for each of them? And if so, why? That alone made it personal, it bound them together, and yet all three men were so different.

Then there were the suspects. Heather was tied to Doug and Nate, and chances were I'd find a connection to Rusty. Public enemy number two was Candice who still had ties to every guy in town and could have befriended Heather as an alibi to cover her ass if suspicion rose against her. On the night Doug was killed, she made sure everyone was in the ballroom. Had it all been an elaborate scheme to make it appear she'd been there the entire time?

On my list of less likely suspects was Rosalind, Doug's mother. She was hiding something, but was a bit up in years to deliver death by knife in one blow to grown men. I didn't put it past her to hire an accomplice to do her bidding for her, but to kill her own son? I didn't think so.

I thought back to the surveillance video. The killer hadn't been able to lift Doug over the side on the first try or the second—my first clue I may have been profiling a woman. But what caused such rage? Only two possibilities came to mind: Jealousy or revenge. And then there was my biggest question. How many more men would die before the killer was finished?

CHAPTER 23

"Morning. Mind if I come in?" I said.

I strolled through the door Candice had just opened.

Candice turned in my direction, but left the door wide open. "I do mind. You're not welcome here."

"Why?" I said eyeballing various personal possessions in her hotel room. "It's not like this is your house."

"I'm paying for the room, same thing."

"Relax," I said. "I won't be here long."

She brushed past me wearing nothing but a men's V-neck t-shirt—minus the bra—and thong panties. I'd never understood how a thin piece of fabric wedged between a woman's crack was considered comfortable enough to endure hours of poking and prodding. I'd tried them myself on a few occasions, but it never took long for me to buckle under the pressure of a never-ending wedgie that sent me running for a pair of thigh-hugging cotton bikinis.

Candice clutched her throat like she was afraid I'd try to

choke the life out of her—again.

I laughed. "This isn't that type of visit."

With her hand still secured over her neck, she said, "Why don't I bhh...believe you?"

"Funny choice of words."

"Why?"

"I'm here because I don't believe *you.*"

She poured a glass of white wine, gulped the entire thing down, and leaned against the wall like it had the ability to offer her some type of protection. She used the empty glass as a pointer finger. "You know what you're like? A teeny tiny gnat buzz...buzz...buzzing in my face, and no matter how many times I'ze swat at it, I can't seem-ze to get it to go away."

"Isn't it a bit early to be drinking?" I said. "You're slurring your words. How much have you had?"

"I've earned the right to do as please—it's called being an adult."

Too bad she didn't know how to act like one.

"Not everything is about you, Candice. I'm here to talk about your relationship with Nate."

She snickered. "Why, you want to date him or something? He's all yours, honey."

"I thought the two of you were supposed to go on vacation together?"

She refilled her glass to the brim and took a nice big gulp. "That was before I caught him wizz another woman at his house in his bed—the same bed we'd shared together the night before."

I sat in a chair next to the only window in the room. "But you're married. So why the hell do you care what he does—wasn't it just some kind of fling?"

"My marriage sucks the only life I have left out of me." Candice pinched her fingers together, pressed them into her lips and then pulled backward like she was trying to extract words from it. "Sucks it out. Sucks it all owwwt."

I shrugged. "So divorce."

She fondled the stem of her glass with her fingers but didn't respond.

"Ah, that's right.," I said. "You can't, can you? You're waiting for the old man to kick it so you can get your hands on his millions."

She rolled her eyes. "You're such a bitch, Sloane. In high school you were the same way. You never even talked to me."

"We didn't know each other back then," I said.

"Correction. You existed, I didn't."

And the insecure little girl comes out to play.

I laughed. "There wasn't a person in school who didn't know you."

She tried to make a face, but her past and most likely

continual use of Botox only allowed her one-and-a-half expressions, which made her look like an impartial woman living in Switzerland. Either way, the constant huffing noise she made after each gulp of wine made it apparent she didn't want me to be there.

"So, you left your posh digs and returned here to date a local?" I said. "Kinda pathetic, don't you think?"

She sucked on the top part of her lip until it disappeared inside her mouth. "It doesn't matter now. I've ruins thingzz between us."

"Then you *did* have feelings for Nate?" I said. "That's why you couldn't handle seeing him with another girl. It crushed you, and you rammed into his car to teach him a lesson."

It made me wonder if she had the song "Before He Cheats" blaring through her car speakers at the moment of impact. She certainly was crazy.

Candice shot her body forward and stumbled while going for the empty bottle of wine. "Rats!" she said, tipping it over. Only it came out *razz*. She stumbled around like she'd just stepped on a wasp.

"Why don't you sit down for a minute?" I said.

She flopped her head back and forth like her neck lacked the support it needed to sustain its weight. "I'll do's what I'z please, and you juss stop trying to get me all…get me all…all…"

I caught her arm before she crashed to the floor and swooped her onto the bed. She mumbled something and then buried her face in a pillow and fell asleep.

Great, now what am I supposed to do?

Although Candice was far from being one of my most favorite people, my first thought was to cover her up, more to shield myself from her exposed flesh than anything else. When I lifted the sheet, I noticed a tattoo on her upper thigh of an exotic blue flower. It was only about two inches long, but the detail was so vivid, it looked real. And if it had been done by Rusty—they had a connection. All three men dead, all with a connection to Candice. Rejection was a strong motivator to kill.

***

A half hour later a grumpy, groggy Candice woke to a vision of me sitting straight up in the bed next to her dangling a knife in my hand.

"What the—where did you…?"

"Get this?" I said, my eyes fastened on the knife. "It's yours, you should know."

"How'd you find it?"

"Hiding something like this inside of a pillowcase on the

bed is a little obvious."

She reached for it and missed. "Give it back—it's mine!"

"Not until you tell me why you have it. Or even better; why don't you tell me who you're planning on killing next so I can stop you?"

"Next?"

"Well Doug's dead, and Rusty, and Nate, so…"

"Is that some kind of joke?"

I leaned in. "Am I laughing?"

"What do you mean, *Nate*? He's fine. He's vacationing without me—probably with that trampy girl he was with the other night."

"The vacation *you* were supposed to be on with him," I said.

"I thought I'd let him see what life was like without me."

"So that's why you didn't go?" I said.

She shrugged. "Why else?"

"When did you see him last?"

"The night I ran into his car."

"Which was?"

She stood up and held out her hands as if to say 'that's enough!'

"I'm sick of all the questions—get out!"

I grabbed her arms and stared her down. "Candice—Nate is dead. He was found in his bed with a knife through the chest, just like Doug, just like Rusty. And you've got a knife hidden in your room, so start talking."

But she didn't. And it became clear she hadn't heard anything I'd said beyond the *Nate's dead* part.

Several minutes went by before she snapped out of the daze she was in and said, "Nate isn't dead...he can't be."

"To be honest, I'm surprised Heather hasn't told you. She works at the hospital. I bet she knows."

"Heather and I don't talk much anymore."

"The way she describes it, the two of you are friends."

She laughed. "You know what's sad? Heather looked like a homely wallflower six months ago. I saw her one night at dinner and felt bad for her. I offered to teach her everything I knew."

Lucky girl.

"So what happened?"

"Not what—who. Doug."

"What do you mean?" I said.

"She could have gone for any guy in town. But not him. Doug was off limits."

"I heard you challenged her to get him in bed just to see if she could do it."

"Never! He was mine."

It was getting weirder by the second. "Doug was Trista's—what's with all this *mine* talk?"

"I don't mean *actually* mine. He was *the one*. You know? The one who got away."

"So why do you have a knife?"

"I was going to ahh…slash Nate's tires. Teach him another lesson."

"The same lesson you taught me?" I said. "Or did you want to even the score after what happened on the cruise?"

"I don't know what you're talking about."

"So you don't know about the note attached to the door of my hotel room, and you didn't flatten my tires?"

"I swear, it wasn't me…what day did it happen?"

"Tuesday."

"I was with Nate all day."

"Convenient alibi seeing how he's no longer with us to…"

"I didn't do it—and don't even try pinning those murders on me! What reason would I have to hurt any of them?"

"I can think of several."

I stood up and walked to the door, knife still in hand. "Stay put for a few days. Or don't," I said. "Either way, I *will* find you."

CHAPTER 24

I exited Candice's hotel room and returned to the parking lot. A shiny black car with blacked-out windows was parked a few stalls away from my own. I walked over to the driver-side window of the vehicle and tapped on it, but nothing happened. I knocked again. There was no movement, but that didn't mean the car was empty.

"Lucio, are you going to put the window down, or what?" I said.

The window lowered.

We locked eyes. "Babysitting again?" I said.

He shook his head. "Nah, it's not like that, Sloane—really. Besides, you and I's friends now, right?"

Over the past month Lucio's bodyguard-like status with Giovanni gave me plenty of time to get to know him on a personal level, but I never thought he regarded me as a friend.

"Look," he said. "You don't want me standing in the way of you doing your thing, I get that. But the boss said to keep an eye on you. If I don't and something happens…" he took his pointer finger and sliced his neck, "Ckkkkt, I'd—"

"Get bumped off, whacked, sent to float around with a sea full of fishes?"

I laughed. He didn't.

"Point is, it makes the boss happy to know you're safe," Lucio said. "He knows you like your space. That's why he didn't send the whole crew—just me."

Crew?

I figured it wouldn't matter what I said. Lucio only took orders from one person, and it wasn't me, so I slid into the passenger side of his car and sat down. "All right 'just me', you wanna tell me what you did to Jesse the other night?"

A wicked smile crossed his face, sending a cold chill up my arms. "Crumb had it comin'…"

"Jesse looks like he was shoved onto the track in the middle of the Kentucky Derby."

Lucio shrugged. "He was still alive when I left him—didn't have to be." He paused. "Why you ask? He givin' you problems again? Because if he is—"

I shook my head. "Jesse's fine. He won't even talk to me."

Lucio turned the key in the ignition and started the car. "Where to, lady?"

With the sun fading into the horizon, we headed to the tattoo parlor. I hoped to gain an audience with Rusty's wife. I was interested to find out if she could make any connections between her husband and the other victims, or with Candice and Heather. Both women seemed to have ties to the other men, but what about Rusty?

Lucio stayed in the car, but he wouldn't remain there long. The moment I walked in, I knew I was out of my element. Way out. There were three tattoo artists, each covered in a variety of different tattoos; one male even had tribal art covering the entire surface of his bicked head.

The door banged closed behind me, and all three people looked over like I'd exited the goodie-goodie express at the wrong stop.

I mustered up a weak smile and did my best to blend in. "I'm looking for Rusty's wife."

A woman in a ribbed black tank top with full sleeves on both arms said, "Yeah, who's askin'?"

"I heard about what happened the other day and I wanted to—"

"Yeah—yeah—yeah—but why are you *here*?" the woman said.

I took a deep breath in. "I take it you were his wife?"

She blinked—twice, but didn't answer.

"Can I ask a few questions?" I said.

She swayed her head toward the chair and eyeballed a nearly-finished tattoo she was working on.

I sat down. "I'll wait."

She waved someone over from the back room, handed off the needle and looked at the barely-legal teenager she was working on. "Kid, take five."

She approached me with her arms crossed and her legs spread like she'd been trained in the military.

"I'm not a reporter or anything," I said.

She waved her hand in the air. "It makes no difference to me who you are—I'll talk, but you'll have to pay."

I pulled my wallet from my bag. "How much?"

"What size?"

"Excuse me?" I said.

"What size do you want?"

I fanned my fingers out in front of me. "You don't understand—I'm not here to get a tattoo."

"Why? You too good for one? Well, maybe I'm too good for you." She pivoted on her bare foot and turned around.

I stood there trying to decide whether a few questions were worth a lifetime of regret. I'd never seriously considered a tattoo of any kind. I wasn't against it; I'd just never loved anything enough to embed it on my body forever. I had two options: I could run, or I could stay, mark myself for life, and possibly get some answers. With all the dead ends around me, I needed a good shove in the right direction.

"Wait…I guess I could get a little something. Let me think about it."

The woman reached behind the counter and grabbed a black binder. "What's your name?" she said.

"Sloane. Yours?"

"Princess Buttercup."

She flopped the book down in front of me, turned around, and all three artists had a good laugh. With her back to me, she said, "Lemme know when you're ready."

I sat down on a worn sofa covered with a faded polka-dot sheet and thumbed through the book. But I didn't look at any of the designs; I pretended for the sake of passing the time. My heart raced and my head pounded, and I considered walking out the door and bagging the idea. And then I remembered my recent phone call to Maddie and her reminder to be the Sloane I was now, and not the one I'd left behind.

The woman finished with the boy and turned to me. "So, what's it gonna be?"

I handed her the book. "Nothing."

"That's what I thought," she said.

"Don't act like you *know* me based on the way I'm dressed or because I came in here thinking I could get somewhere being polite. Today isn't the first time I've considered getting inked, and it isn't my first trip to a tattoo shop either. Three years ago, my sister died, and I've considered celebrating her memory in a variety of ways, but I won't rush it on a dare." I started for the door. "Thanks for your time, Buttercup."

"Wait."

I turned. The expression on her face had softened.

"What was your sister's name?" she said.

"Gabrielle."

She frowned. "What happened, if you don't mind my askin'?"

I did, but given the circumstances, I didn't see how it mattered. "She was killed."

"Accident?"

I shook my head. "Murdered."

She raised a brow. "They catch whoever did it?"

I smiled. "I did, yes."

She stepped back. "What do you mean, *you* did? You a cop?"

"Private investigator."

She shook her head and looked back at me with a new level of respect. "Well, isn't that…huh."

She stood still for several seconds and then pointed to a framed photo on the wall. "My brother, Lee. He died about five years back. Gang shooting in Bakersfield. That's where

I'm from."

I stared at the man in the photo, all the while thinking it wasn't hard to see how he got in that kind of trouble. But family was family no matter what path a person chose. "I'm sorry."

"Yeah, me too." She leaned over and rested her elbows on the counter. "So look—about the tat, forget it. Let's start again. My name is Elise, but everyone calls me Liz. And if you still wanna talk, I'll answer your questions."

I followed her to a back room. Once the door was shut behind us she said, "Go for it."

"Did Rusty ever tattoo Candice Flaherty?"

Liz called Candice a four-letter word that made me cringe every time I heard it.

"He didn't, I did. And if you look close enough, you might be able to see the word tramp etched in the center of it."

It was the perfect lead-in to my next question. "Did Candice and Rusty ever…"

Liz shrugged. "Rusty wasn't the type to keep it in his pants, if you know what I mean."

"And that didn't bother you?" I said.

"He was a mean son of a bitch, but a loveable one."

"Despite his affairs?"

She leaned back against the wall. "Why you so interested

in Candice, anyway?"

"All the men who are dead seem to know her in one way or another."

"Small town. Some days it feels like we're all connected."

"What about Heather Masterson?" I said. "Did Rusty know her?"

She looked up and repeated the name to herself. "Don't think so."

"Did he ever mention Doug or Nate?"

"Not Doug—I never really knew him. Wasn't he the banker guy who died on the cruise ship?"

I nodded. "Rusty played poker with Nate, right?"

She nodded. "Every week."

"Who else? Were there ever any women around?"

She rolled her eyes. "Nate didn't consider it a party unless there was plenty of ass at his place."

"Do you know who specifically?"

She shook her head. "All I cared about was when Rusty was with me, he was with me. I didn't worry about whether he was cheatin' or who he was cheatin' with. At the end of the day, he always came home."

"Did Rusty ever mention the other guys to you—what they talked about—anything?"

"Not really, I didn't ask."

Dead end. Again.

She bent one of her knees and braced her foot against the wall. "You know what—

I think Rusty did mention him to me once."

"Who?"

"Doug."

"When?"

"One night several years back Rusty got drunk—I'm talkin' couldn't-tie-his-own-shoelaces kind of drunk. He didn't like alcohol, and never had it much. Always made him real mean. So that night, it hit him hard. Anyway, he started spouting off about how his buddies all got it on with some girl back in high school at a party."

"What girl—Candice?"

She shrugged. "I dunno, he never said her name. The only reason I remember is because you mentioned Doug."

"Are you saying he was there?"

"According to Rusty he was."

"You're sure he said Doug?"

She nodded.

I was shocked.

"Did he ever mention it again after that night?"

She shook her head. "But he told me the names of the other guys: Nate, Doug and Jesse."

"As in police officer, Jesse?"

She smiled. "That's the one."

CHAPTER 25

The lights at Jesse's house were off when Lucio and I arrived. I knocked on the door, first by tapping on it and then hard enough for his neighbors to hear, but it never opened. I assumed he was still on duty and decided to go back to the hotel and try again later.

When we got out of the car, I turned to Lucio. "You have a room here, I take it?"

He grinned. "Right next to yours."

We neared the door and Lucio pointed at the window. "You leave those on?"

I looked over. A dull light filtered through the sheer curtains inside the room. I shook my head and drew my weapon. Lucio, already two steps ahead of me, shielded my body with his arm.

"Let me go first."

"I'm a big girl," I said. "We can go in together."

The aggravated look on his face stopped me from

arguing further. A figure inside my room walked by the curtain and the light went out.

"Get down," Lucio whispered.

"Don't you need to get down, too?" I said.

Lucio sighed like he didn't know how much longer he could put up with me. We knelt and waited. Nothing happened. There was no movement of any kind; just a faint glow from what I assumed was a flashlight. The thought of someone rifling through my things again entered my mind and didn't exit.

I stood back up. "This is ridiculous. I'm done with people thinking they can invade my privacy. I'm going in."

Lucio pulled me back. "Hold on there, Sloane. We gotta think this through."

I shrugged out of his death grip and faced him. "We've waited long enough. Let's do this."

He looked at me like I was an untamed cat who'd just been sprung from a cage. And I felt like one.

"Boss said you had a little of that uh, OCD, I think they call it."

"He what!"

What else had Giovanni said about me?

"All right," Lucio said, "we'll go in. I go first, you follow." He held a finger up to stop me from saying anything else. "Not a word. We do this my way or not at all."

We approached the door and Lucio touched the handle. "It's unlocked."

He nudged it open, stuck his gun out in front of him, and went in. I followed. The living area was dark except for a faint glimmer of light radiating from the bedroom. We walked eight short steps until we were both standing in front of the door. It was only open a crack, but I could make out the image of a person sitting on the edge of the bed. It looked like a man.

Lucio pointed the gun at the man's back and said, "Get up."

But the man didn't move.

"You deaf, pal? I said get up," Lucio said—again. "Don't make me ask a third time."

"Put the gun down," the man said.

Lucio lowered his weapon and flipped the light switch on.

"Sorry, Boss, I didn't think you'd be back until tomorrow."

He looked at Lucio and then at me. "My business was finished so I returned early."

"What were you doing in here with the lights off?" I said.

He smiled. "Waiting."

"For me?"

As much as I wanted him to say yes, the expression on

his face said something different.

"What's wrong?" I said.

Giovanni got up. "Follow me."

The three of us walked into the living room. Giovanni opened the desk drawer and pulled out two items: A note and a scalpel.

CHAPTER 26

"Leave, or you'll be next…" I read aloud.

"The note was stuck to the door when I got here," Giovanni said.

"Again?" I said. "I'm running out of places to stay in this town."

"It wasn't on the outside of the door."

I swallowed—hard. "It was on the inside?"

Giovanni nodded.

"Someone was in my room?" I said.

"And they wanted you to know it," Giovanni said.

I crossed the room and sat on the sofa.

"Do you know what this is?" Giovanni said picking up the scalpel.

But my eyes were focused on Lucio. In the midst of our conversation, he'd disengaged himself and was running from room to room yanking the curtains closed. Since it was a hotel, there were only three. When the task was finished, he pulled his phone out of his pocket and dialed a number. A few seconds later two more men entered the room.

"Wait a minute," I said. "I thought you were the only member of the *crew* who was here?"

Before anyone had the chance to answer, there was a knock at the door. I stood up, all four men looked at me like they couldn't imagine what I was thinking. In a roomful of male testosterone used to getting their way, I wouldn't be allowed anywhere near the door.

Giovanni looked at Lucio and nodded. Lucio pushed all two hundred seventy-five pounds of himself off the chair and approached the door. The other two guys positioned themselves close by while Giovanni walked over and stood by me. I felt like I was in a hostage situation.

Instead of looking out the peephole, Lucio spoke. "Who's there?"

A female voice on the other side said, "Is this Sloane's room?"

Lucio said, "Who's askin'?"

"Rosalind Ward—Doug's mother. Is this her room or not?"

"It's all right," I said. "I know her."

Lucio opened the door.

Rosalind stepped in, glanced around the room and frowned. "I'm not sure what's going on here, but I need to speak with Ms. Monroe."

No one moved. Rosalind rolled her eyes and tried again. "Privately, if you don't mind."

The men looked at Giovanni and he flicked two fingers. They left, he stayed.

"And you," Rosalind said, looking at Giovanni, "you'll be leaving too, I assume?"

He stood up, walked over, and placed his hand on her shoulder. "I will not."

Rosalind looked at me like I needed to provide her with an explanation.

I smiled. "He ahh...will not. So if you have something to say, Rosalind..."

"All right then, I will. I'd like you to leave town," she said.

"Why?"

"It doesn't matter. I can take care of Doug's wife myself. We don't need your help, so there's no reason for you to stay."

"Trista's a much stronger woman than she realizes. She's doing a fine job on her own," I said.

Rosalind looked at me with a glimmer of hope.

"So you'll do it then—you'll leave?"

"Why are you so anxious to get me out of here?"

She pressed her pants down with her hand like she was trying to get the wrinkles out. "I don't get anxious. My family has been through enough. I'd convinced Alexa to take a leave from school, and she was all set until you interfered."

"You want me to leave because I talked to Alexa? Or is there something more?"

Her nose wrinkled. "I don't know what you're suggesting, but I don't care for it."

Giovanni, who was now standing by the desk, grabbed the note and held it out in front of Rosalind. "Do you wish Sloane to leave bad enough you would threaten her?"

Rosalind snatched the paper from his hand and looked it over. "I didn't have anything to do with this—where did you get it?"

"Seems you're not the only one uncomfortable with my presence," I said.

She waved the note in the air. "All the more reason you should leave."

I stood up and placed my hands on my hips. "I'm not going anywhere."

"I haven't even made it worth your while yet."

I laughed. "Not everyone can be bought with money."

The comment seemed to surprise both Rosalind and Giovanni alike. But a smug-faced Rosalind didn't allow it to affect her mission. "What if you could name your price?"

I gave it some thought. "All right then."

"How much?"

"I don't want your money."

"What then—a gift of some kind? Name it."

"Justice."

Her eyes narrowed. "I don't follow."

"I'll leave when Doug's killer is found and pays for his or her crimes—and not a moment before."

CHAPTER 27

While Giovanni spoke to his men in the kitchenette, I paced the bedroom. There was a good reason why Rosalind wanted me gone, and I needed to find it. Alexa was a hot button with her, so I decided to start there. I sat on a chair next to a circular table, connected my laptop to the internet and searched the name Alexa Ward on the Archives website. It didn't take long for me to access her birth certificate.

Born Alexandria Anne Ward on December 28, 1991, it wasn't hard to do the math. Trista would have gotten pregnant before graduation, which was the reason they dropped out of college and got married. But why hide it? Wasn't it obvious the baby in the baby carriage came first? The certificate listed the parents as Doug and Trista Ward, no surprises there, and the doctor as Wayne F. Robinson, MD, a name I knew well. He was the same doctor who delivered me.

Giovanni entered the room with a curious look on his

face. "What are you staring at so intently?"

"Alexa's birth certificate. She's Trista's daughter," I said.

"Why are you so interested?"

"I don't know yet. She's a sore spot with Rosalind every time we talk to each other. According to the birth certificate, Alexa was conceived before Trista and Doug married, but Trista hasn't said a word to me; in fact, no one has."

"How they came to be parents doesn't seem relevant to the murders. Maybe she wanted to keep that part of her life private."

I wasn't so sure.

CHAPTER 28

The home Wayne F. Robinson, MD resided in was a square, single-level structure that looked like it had been built back in the time of covered wagons and hoop skirts. Green shutters with chipped paint adorned the windows on all sides of the red brick house.

I ascended a few steps and knocked. From the see-through glass etching in the center of the door someone inside the house rose from a chair and glanced in my direction. It was a man. He stretched his hand out, grabbed something at his side and began what would become a two minute trek to the front door. When it finally opened, I was shocked at the man who stood before me. He was hunched over and now used a cane. His once slick brown hair had been replaced with strands of white, and he was a foot or two shorter than I remembered.

"Doctor Robinson?" I said.

He smiled revealing a mouth with eighty percent of its

teeth still intact. "Yes?"

"I don't know if you remember me," I said. "Sloane Monroe. You delivered my sister and me in the seventies."

He rubbed a finger across his chin. "Twins?"

I nodded, shocked his memory was still so vivid.

"You girls were the only babies that came out the way you did," he said.

"How's that?"

"Jet black hair. Both of you. Never seen so much hair on two babies before. Is there something I can do for you?"

"I wanted to ask you about another baby you delivered."

He swung the door open and winked. "I'm not sure how much help I'll be, but I never turn down the opportunity for a little company."

I followed him past a bevy of hanging plants and sat in a chair at the kitchen table. He retrieved two glasses from the cupboard and set one down in front of me.

"What can I get you?" he said. "Milk? Juice? Water? And if you don't like any of those, I can brew some coffee."

"I'm fine."

"How about some orange juice?"

To send the conversation in a non-liquid direction, I smiled and nodded.

The good doctor returned seconds later and joined me. "Now, what is it you wanted to talk to me about?"

"Twenty years ago you delivered a baby for Doug and Trista Ward."

The ice in the glass he held rattled.

"Is everything okay?" I said.

He mustered a slight grin. "Fine...fine."

But it wasn't fine. The moment I mentioned their names his eyes darted around the room like a fly with no place to land.

"Why do you want to know about the baby?" he said.

I sipped my drink. "Alexa's birth was kept quiet from what I understand. I looked through the archived newspapers this morning. There wasn't even an announcement about her arrival. Don't you find that strange?

He leaned back in his chair. "Why?"

"This is Rosalind Ward's grandbaby we're talking about here. Her *first* grandbaby. Alexa should have made her debut on the front page."

He shook his head. "How would I know anything?"

"Doug's sons, Joshua and Jack, had a full-page spread on page one. Care to know who joined them in the photo?"

He frowned.

"Rosalind," I said. "She glammed it up for the camera with that ridiculous smile of hers and a little bundle of joy in each one of her arms."

He turned his hand upward. "There's not much to say. I delivered Alexa, and I was her pediatrician as a child. Beyond that, there's not much I can tell you about her. I'm sorry you came all this way for nothing."

Nice try, but his hand hadn't stopped shaking.

"I've had Alexa on my mind a lot over the past few days," I said. "Something about her has bothered me since the moment we met. For a Ward, she has a weird shaped head."

He stifled a laugh. "What do you mean?"

"Doug had a square-shaped head, so does Trista, so do the twin boys, but Alexa has an oval—a very defined oval."

"So?"

"Two squares don't produce an oval, do they? And what about those blue eyes of hers? Doug's were brown, the same as Trista and the boys. Do you see where I'm going with all this yet?"

He made a gurgling sound once, then again, and looked me in the eye. "Listen to me very carefully, Sloane. I'm not sure why you're looking into the past, but it would be best if you didn't." He waved his hand back and forth. "Forget about this nonsense."

"Best for whom?"

"What?"

"You just said it would be best if I didn't look into the past," I said. "Why?"

"Sometimes it's better if things remain as they are."

I'd grown tired of everyone's excuses. He knew something. It was obvious.

"I'm not leaving town until I find out what it is no one will tell me. If I have to go back to Rosalind and force it out of her, I will."

He hung his head and whispered, "I wish you wouldn't."

The egg had almost cracked. If I pushed a little harder, I was confident he'd tell me what I needed to know. I slammed my hand down on the table but not hard enough to give him a heart attack. "How many men need to die before someone in this town breaks their silence!"

"I don't understand. What do the murders have to do with Alexa?"

"You tell me."

A perfect mixture of sorrow and regret covered his face. "If I tell you what I know, I need to be sure Rosalind doesn't find out it came from me. You don't understand what it's like to live in this town with her watching your every move. I'm finally under her radar after all these years, and I won't get sucked back into her world—not again."

"No one will ever know it was you. I promise."

He relaxed a little but still looked like he was in fear over what he was about to tell me. "Many years ago, Rosalind came to me with a request. She said Doug had gotten a girl pregnant."

If the girl had been the mysterious woman from the party, how would anyone have known the baby belonged to Doug and not one of the other guys?

"What was the girl's name?"

"I don't recall."

"Can't you look it up?" I said.

He shook his head. "There's no paperwork."

"Why?"

"Rosalind thought the girl was lying, but she didn't want to take any chances. When the girl went into labor, Rosalind brought her to me. And once the baby was born, a DNA test was performed. There was no doubt—the baby was Doug's."

"Alexa was the baby, right?"

He nodded.

"I don't understand," I said. "You're saying the mother just handed her baby over to Doug and Trista?"

He tilted his head to the side. "Not exactly."

"Well then, what happened?"

"We…no…I …told the mother the baby died shortly after it was born. It was a good way to keep the mother away from her baby until we were sure whose baby it was."

I felt like my lungs had collapsed. "Why would you do such a thing?"

"It was Rosalind…you don't understand, I had to."

"How much did she pay you to keep quiet?" I said. "And there's no use telling me she didn't bribe you for your services…I know better."

"Fifty."

"Thousand?"

His silence provided the answer.

So much was being revealed, I couldn't keep up. "Let me make sure I have this right. A girl gets pregnant and Doug is the father. The baby, who I know as Alexa, is born, and the mother is told the baby died shortly after she gave birth. Why wouldn't she want to see her baby one last time or plan a funeral for it?"

"You underestimate Rosalind's power. The girl was paid handsomely to keep her mouth shut. She agreed to leave town and never return or get in touch with Doug again. It was understood Rosalind would be in charge of the funeral arrangements."

"Of course it was. But what I don't understand is how none of this ever got out?"

"The only people in the room besides me were Rosalind and Doug."

"It doesn't change the facts. A baby was born, and that baby grew up in this town. You're telling me no one noticed Trista wasn't pregnant and then all of the sudden had a baby?"

"The young lady found out she was pregnant in her first trimester. Once Rosalind got involved, her only goal was damage control. Rosalind moved Trista into her house, and for six months, Trista wasn't seen by anyone. No one knew she wasn't the mother of the baby. Not even her parents."

I pushed myself out of the chair and stood. Doctor Robinson tried to do the same, but it took far more effort for him to get to his feet.

"I need to go," I said.

He placed his hand on my arm. "You must understand. I didn't think I was doing anything wrong. The girl was a mess. Some druggie teenager with a bad home life from Lancaster. She wasn't in any condition to raise a baby. I gave Alexa the best chance for a decent life."

He'd played God, but one look in his eyes and I could tell he knew it wasn't right. I opened the front door and stepped onto the porch. "It wasn't for you to decide."

The web of lies I'd been fed had spun out of control, and on the top of the list was one person: Trista.

CHAPTER 29

Screams echoed from inside the house. I didn't bother knocking—I forced the door open and ran inside. The foyer was empty, and there was no sign of Trista or the kids. Another scream sounded and I rushed toward the master bedroom. I thought about signaling Lucio who waited for me in the car, but there wasn't time. I drew my gun, braced myself against the wall and slid down the hallway, trying to make the smallest sound possible. I entered the bedroom and heard voices. Trista spoke and then someone else, but it was muffled, and I couldn't make it out until I moved closer.

"Stop it!" Trista shouted.

I rounded the corner, prepared for anything, but the scene wasn't what I imagined. One of the twin boys sat on the bathroom counter, blood seeping from his knee. Trista hunched over him. Each time she rubbed the cotton ball over his wound, he made a high-pitched squeal. It reminded me of a kid strapped into a roller coaster ride he never wanted to go on in the first place. I tried to stow my gun back in the holster, but I was too late.

Alexa saw me first and said, "Did you just have a gun pointed at us?"

"Wow," the uninjured twin shouted. "Awesome!"

I looked at Trista. "I'm so sorry, it's just…I thought…well, your son, he sounded like…"

"A scared little girl?" the uninjured twin said. He elbowed his brother and cracked up with laughter. "Told ya so, baby!"

The injured twin crossed his arms and stuck his bottom lip out.

"That's not what I was going to say," I lied. "I thought someone was hurt."

Alexa slipped by me and whispered, "Good save."

"Accident?" I said.

Trista made a face like she was preparing for a 'you're grounded' type of lecture and pointed at the injured twin. "This one was wearing roller blades in the kitchen."

I leaned over and assessed the injury. "Ouch."

"You should see the wall he ran into," Trista said. "It needs repair worse than he does."

I waited for Trista to finish and invited her to join me for a walk. We went outside and walked by Lucio. He nodded. I nodded back.

"Who's that?" Trista said.

"Nobody," I said. "Why didn't you tell me the truth about Alexa?"

"What truth?"

"I know what happened the night she was born—and about the other woman."

Her body stiffened. "Who told you?"

"It doesn't matter," I said. "I understand why you kept it from me, but something about it makes me feel like what happened is tied to the murders."

"How?"

"Did Doug ever tell you about the night the girl got pregnant?"

"He didn't, Rosalind did. She said Doug was drunk at some party and the girl took advantage of him."

"She didn't say anything else?"

Trista shook her head. "Why?"

"What made you claim Alexa as your own? Did Rosalind pay you?"

Trista stopped. "Excuse me?"

"Did she offer you money?"

"I can't believe you just asked me that."

"I didn't say you took it, I just wondered if it was offered."

"It wasn't!"

"So why'd you do it?"

She sighed. "Can we sit?"

We found a spot by the curb.

"I said no at first," she said.

"You must have been angry."

"And humiliated. Doug sent his mother to talk to me—he didn't have the nerve to tell me himself. Can you believe it? And then she sat there and expected me to comply with the plans she'd made, no questions asked."

I crossed one leg over the other. "What did she say, exactly?"

"Everything would be all right if I did what she wanted."

"And if you didn't?"

"She made it clear; my relationship with Doug would be over. Rosalind said she wasn't sure the baby was even Doug's and thought the woman was just some gold digger, but until she knew for sure, she wanted me to move into their house until the baby was born and everything could be sorted out."

Usually whenever a prolonged moment of silence passed, I found it awkward to sit there and keep quiet. But there was an element of hurt and regret to Trista's words, and I found myself sympathetic rather than judgmental. If anyone was to blame, it was Rosalind and Doug for allowing his mother to clean up his mess. But he was gone, so it was far too late for a lecture. Rosalind, on the other hand, was someone I was more than happy to put under pressure. She needed to know what it felt like to be on the opposite end for once.

"Alexa is *my* daughter," Trista said. "I love her like I love my boys. She doesn't know any of this."

"I won't be the one to tell her," I said. "Alexa's already lost a father; she doesn't need to lose you too."

"I just don't understand why you think any of this pertains to Doug."

"I don't either—not yet anyway."

A tear dropped from the corner of her eye and she turned away.

"I'm sorry to ask this, but it's important. What do you know about Alexa's mother?"

"Not much. I never even met her."

"What about her name?"

Trista shook her head. "Rosalind said the girl didn't want the baby, and all I cared about was Doug not being humiliated when everyone in town found out what he had done."

Out of confusion came the clarity I'd been seeking for more than a week: A suspect and a motive. All that remained was finding out who Alexa's real mother was and whether two decades of suppressed anger made her crazy enough to kill.

CHAPTER 30

I stopped by Jesse's house a second time, but still no cigar. And since he refused my texts and phone calls, my only option was to catch up with him in person. After the bomb Rusty dropped on his wife about the group sexcapade, combined with the revelation of how Alexa was conceived, Jesse was the only man still alive to tell about it. But if my theory was correct, there was one gaping hole in it: Why wouldn't the killer go after Rosalind too?

I needed to know more so I called Rosalind and arranged to meet at my hotel. She was hesitant until I sweetened the deal by promising I'd leave town afterward. That little carrot was too enticing for her to pass up, and it wasn't a lie per se. I had every intention of leaving—once I'd solved the case.

**

Rosalind drove a pearl-colored Rolls Royce into the parking

lot. It was so nice I expected it to come complete with a built-in chauffeur. But she exited alone. Of course, no one in Tehachapi needed an escort, but if there was ever a person who could find an excuse, it was Rosalind. I approached, and she glanced around like she expected to find a handful of eavesdroppers hanging on to every word.

"I thought we were talking in your room?" she said.

"It's a nice day; I thought we could meet outside."

She turned her nose up to the idea.

"If you want to go to my hotel room, we can, but you should know there are a few men camped out in there, and this time you'd be speaking in front of everyone."

She slung a leather bag over her shoulder and sighed. "Follow me."

We walked into the lobby of the hotel and approached the front desk. A young girl with French-braided hair and pink braces blinked her eyes and said, "How can I help you ladies?"

"I need to speak to the manager," Rosalind said.

"Maybe I can help," the girl said.

Rosalind wasn't amused. "The manager—please."

A man emerged from the corner office, took one look at Rosalind and straightened his tie. He attempted to pull up his sagging pants, but they fell back down again. "Mrs. Ward," he said, "nice to see you."

She offered him a I'm-smiling-because-I-need-something look. It was one she gave often. "I need a place we can talk," she said motioning to me. "Somewhere we won't be disturbed."

"I believe the meeting room down the hall is empty."

He checked to be sure and then closed the door behind us.

Rosalind sat down. "I'm glad you've decided to leave. A wise choice. Now why did you need to see me?"

I smiled.

"I want to know about the woman Doug slept with in high school."

She glared at me. "What are you talking about?"

I pulled the folded up birth certificate out of my pocket, opened it, and handed it over. "I'm talking about *this.*"

She studied it for a moment. "Why come to me when you can go to Trista yourself?"

"Not Trista," I said, "the other woman—Alexa's birth mother."

She rubbed her hand over her chest like she'd just experienced a sharp pain.

"I'm a private investigator, Mrs. Ward. I do this for a living. If you refuse to answer my questions, I'll stay indefinitely. I'm sure you've kept your share of secrets over the years. Do you really want me to uncover them all?"

"Who told you?"

"It doesn't matter."

She drummed her fingernails in sequence on the table. "I assure you, it does to me."

"I need a name, Mrs. Ward."

"I suppose it wouldn't do me any good to lie about it now. It seems you've got some kind of proof the birth mother exists, but you have no reason to search for her after all this time. I've taken every precaution to ensure she never found out about Alexandria."

"Paying her off isn't a guarantee."

"The girl has no reason to suspect her child ever lived."

Once she realized the revelation she'd just exposed, her hand flew to her mouth.

I relaxed back in my chair. Finally, a simple truth had been revealed.

"Relax; you just confirmed what I already know. How could you allow Trista to think the baby was unwanted for all these years?"

"What did you tell her?"

"Nothing…yet," I said. "I wanted to get all the facts straight first, but if you don't make it right with her, I will."

Through clenched teeth she spouted, "I saved that child's life! All I could think about was what kind of life my precious Alexa would have had if I hadn't stepped in. I wasn't about to let some scared pill-popping girl take off with *my* granddaughter."

"But saying her baby is dead—isn't that taking it too far, even for you?"

"You said you came here to find out what happened to Doug, but so far you've only managed to tear apart my family. If you reveal what you know, you'll hurt the one person who's innocent."

"My goal isn't to ruin Alexa's life, but I want the truth, and you're the one person who can give it to me."

Rosalind intertwined her fingers and rested them on the edge of the table. "If I reveal the name of Alexa's birth mother, do I have your word you won't share what you know with anyone?"

I thought about the promise I'd already made to Trista. But part of me imagined myself at Alexa's age. I'd want to know, but would she feel the same? I had no way of knowing how the truth would affect her.

"I'll keep quiet for now, but only because I don't believe the truth should come from me. Now, I want a name."

"Ivy West."

I wrote it down.

"Don't get all excited thinking you're going to find her. She disappeared years ago," Rosalind said. "No good will come from digging up the past now. We've all moved on."

CHAPTER 31

I returned to my hotel room and searched the internet for the name Ivy West. Her birth certificate was easy to find, nothing exciting there. I jotted down the name of her parents and her date of birth which made her my senior by three months.

The online databases I tried provided little information until I came across a newspaper article published in 1992. Ivy had been listed as missing, but her parents claimed she wasn't kidnapped, she was just a runaway. According to their statement, Ivy had threatened to leave multiple times and said if she did, they'd never see her again. From what the article said, her parents had no interest in finding her, and without her parents support, it didn't take long for the case to go cold.

At the end of the article, I clicked on a link and was sent to the FBI's National Crime Information Center. The page contained two photos of Ivy, both taken as a teenager. Her wavy blond hair fell past her shoulders, but that wasn't what stood out the most. It was her eyes. The same piercing baby blues Alexa had. In the photos, Ivy was around the same age Alexa was now—they looked like twins. The more I stared at the photo, the more the girl staring back didn't remind me of a killer. She looked like a scared young girl looking for a way out.

Under the remarks section, it stated Ivy had dropped out of high school and was working at a local yogurt shop at the time of her disappearance. I scrolled down the page until I came to a section called THE DETAILS. It stated the following:

Ivy West left her home in Lancaster, California on the morning of February 21, 1992 for her job at the local yogurt shop in town. Her co-worker reported she never showed up for work, and she didn't return home that evening. West's parents stated she took the bus every day, but the bus driver was certain she wasn't at the bus stop when he arrived to pick her up. She was last seen wearing a white t-shirt, jeans, and Keds shoes. She also had on a gold heart-shaped locket which she always wore on her wrist.

Had Ivy used the money from Rosalind to skip town forever, and if so, where had she been hiding all this time?

CHAPTER 32

The town of Lancaster was forty-seven miles up Tehachapi-Willow Springs Road. The drive itself offered plenty of scenery to passing motorists. The Tehachapi Wind Farm provided one of the most spectacular views with its showcase of over a thousand windmills, also called wind turbines, hovering some five hundred feet in the air. Passing the big white pinwheels was something even a person like Giovanni wouldn't soon forget. But as fascinated as he was, nothing prepared him for what came next: The Willow Springs International Raceway.

"It's wonderful to see something this amazing out here," he said.

"When I tell people where I grew up they can't even pronounce it, let alone understand what compels a person to live here. Most aren't aware we have places like the raceway and Edwards Air Force Base in the area."

The conversation switched to trains and the history of

the Tehachapi Loop and didn't wrap up until we reached our destination at 592 Lakeshore Road. My expectation of the living conditions we'd find was blown when we drove up. Instead of a single-wide manufactured home in a rundown trailer park, I found myself looking over an immaculately kept Victorian charmer.

In the front yard, a woman raked leaves into a black plastic bag. She spotted us and leaned her rake against the tree.

"Can I help you with something?" she said.

"Mrs. West?"

She shook her head. "No, Anne Thomas."

"Sorry," I said, "I was told Ivy West's parents lived here."

"They used to—not anymore though. I bought the place a few years back." She rested her hands on her hips. "You should have seen it. This is what two years of renovations looks like. I never thought this house would ever come alive again, but I can't complain about the way it turned out."

I looked at Giovanni. "I guess we came all this way for nothing."

Anne removed the rubber gloves she was wearing and swished her fingers back and forth in the air allowing them to dry.

"If you don't mind, can I ask why you're interested in the West's?" she said.

"I was just trying to get some information." I reopened the car door. "Thanks for your time."

"Hold on a second. What kind of information?"

"It's probably best not to discuss it unless it's with Mr. or Mrs. West."

"Mr. West has been gone for years now, so you won't find him."

I leaned on the car door. "How do you know?"

"Because…I'm Mrs. West's sister."

Giovanni and I shared a look like maybe the trip hadn't been a waste of time after all and then we walked over to where Anne was standing.

"Where is Mrs. West?" I said.

Anne swung her finger back and forth between Giovanni and me.

"I'd rather know who you two are first if you don't mind."

"I'm a private investigator looking into the disappearance of your niece, Ivy."

"You're wasting your time," she said. "Ivy's been gone so long, no one cares anymore. Why bother?"

"I have my reasons. Can you tell me where I might find your sister?"

She winked and said, "Come with me."

We followed her inside the house and over to the

fireplace. She titled her head toward the mantle. "There she is."

"She's dead?" I said.

Anne nodded. "Car accident, been two years now."

"I'm sorry."

She shrugged. "We were never that close, to be honest. But I guess I had the best relationship with her out of everyone in the family."

"Would you mind if I asked you a few questions about Ivy's disappearance?"

She shrugged. "Fine by me—but I don't know much."

"Did you know Ivy was pregnant?"

"Her parents wanted her to have an abortion, but she was determined to have that baby. Planned on raising it herself, too."

"And no one thought it was strange when she didn't come home with it?"

"Ivy spouted off one thing one day and something else the next. Said she changed her mind at the last minute—didn't want to talk about it. We assumed she gave it up for adoption."

"And none of you were with her when she had the baby?"

"When she refused to get an abortion, her parents said they didn't want anything to do with it. Truth was, they didn't have the money to take care of Ivy, let alone a newborn. I wanted to be there for her, but I didn't even find out she'd had it until after the baby was born."

"Did she ever say who the father was?"

"All Ivy said was she didn't know. Could have been any number of guys."

Up to that point, Ivy's aunt had been a straight shooter, and there was nothing in her body language to indicate she was lying. The more I thought about Ivy, the more I felt for her, which made me uneasy. Why was I sympathizing with a possible cold-blooded killer? Some weird nurturing instinct had taken root inside me, and I had the sudden urge to find her and give back the life that was so hastily taken away.

"Do you know anything about the day Ivy went missing?" I said.

"My sister called me, crying. Said she thought Ivy'd run off because they'd had a horrible fight the night before."

"What about?"

"Ivy came home rambling about how she felt the stress they put on her about getting rid of the baby hurt the baby in some way. I didn't see how it mattered since she decided not to keep it."

Or killed it. At least in Ivy's mind. It made sense. If only she knew.

CHAPTER 33

I had a hunch Jesse had been the master of secrets, perhaps concealing even more than Rosalind. So I returned to his place again, but this time, I didn't care how long I had to wait. When he came home, I'd be there.

Taped to Jesse's front window was a vinyl sign suggesting the house was being monitored by some kind of security company. But on a scale from one to ten, the home fell in the too-old-and-rundown-why-bother range. And I imagined a burglar would view it as a waste of time. There were two possible scenarios: One, I broke in and found out the sign was nothing more than a prop, or two, I broke in and an alarm went off, thereby alerting Jesse and various others of a possible break-in. Either way, I was past the point of giving a damn. I was going inside.

Jesse's front door was locked when I tried it, but the back door wasn't. One twist of the knob and I was in. And unless the alarm was silent, nothing happened. The inside of his house was even smaller than it appeared on the outside. And brown. Everything from the bedding to the dusty cobwebs in the windows was a different shade of brown. From the looks of things, he'd knocked out the wall to the only bedroom and turned the place into a studio adorned with beer bottles and football-player bobble heads. It was every man's dream and every woman's worst nightmare.

I poked around in a few drawers, but only found proof of Jesse's minimalist lifestyle. There were no notes, scraps of paper or anything to tell me more about him than I already knew. Even his closet was bare except for the essentials.

Once I was confident my snooping skills provided all there was to see, I plopped down on the sofa and waited. An hour went by, and then two. Somewhere between drifting off to sleep and the third hour, headlights beamed through Jesse's windows signaling my wake-up call. A car door slammed shut, and footsteps shuffled up the front stairs. A key was inserted into the door and the living room filled with light.

Jesse took one look at me and made a growling sound that sounded more animalistic than human.

"Uh, surprise?" I said.

"Uh, breaking and entering? You ever heard of it?"

The swelling on his bruised face had gone down—a little, but not a lot.

"Been caught a few times," I said. "You're looking at a

pro."

"Yeah—well, I don't know how you got in here, or..."

"Back door," I said and pointed. "You really should lock both doors when you leave and keep your, uh, security system turned on. That's some high tech piece of cardboard you got there."

He wasn't amused.

"Look," I said, "you wouldn't answer my texts or my phone calls. What else was I supposed to do? I have a home somewhere else, and I'd like to get back to it one day."

He turned his back to me.

"I'm not leaving until you answer my questions," I said.

"If I wanted to answer them, I would have called back. What does that tell you?"

"I need information, Jesse. Tell me what I want to know and I'll never bother you again."

He opened the fridge, grabbed a Dr. Pepper and hovered for a moment like he was trying to make a decision.

"Ask your questions, but it doesn't mean I'll answer 'em," he said. "It just means I want this over with and you gone."

It was better than nothing.

"Did you know about Alexa?"

He plopped down on a recliner and snapped the tab back on the can of soda. "You're gonna have to give me a little more," he said.

"All right. Did you know about the other woman? Alexa's *real* mother."

He flicked the metal cap on the Dr. Pepper several times with his fingernail and then said, "Yes."

"How did you know her?"

"I was the one who introduced them."

"At the party?"

He raised a brow. "How'd you know?"

"Doug, Nate, Rusty—they're all dead and you're alive. What do you think that means?"

"Nothin'. It doesn't mean a damn thing."

"The four of you passed Ivy West around like she was a bucket of popcorn. And why not—it was fun, right? Until she showed up a couple months later pregnant, looking for the baby daddy. I'd guess the fun and games were over at that point, right?"

Jesse sprung from his chair and leaned over me like he wanted to bend me over his knee and teach me a lesson. "I wanna know right now who you've been talkin' to, Sloane."

"No!"

"Yes!"

"Back off me, Jesse."

"Or what?"

"Come closer and find out."

He let out a deep belly laugh and wagged a finger at

me. "You're funny, you know? Not many girls out there like you anymore."

"Last time I checked I was a one-of-a-kind."

He backed a couple feet away and towered over me, arms folded. "So now what?"

But he wasn't looking at me when he said it.

I glanced at a shrine of beer bottles lined up in a row on a corner bookcase. "Why do you keep staring at that bottle?" I said.

"I aint starin' at no bottle."

"You were," I said. "The one in the middle—the BUD LIGHT."

I took a step toward the bottle, but before I could grip it in my hand, Jesse had something pointed at me, and it wasn't his finger.

"Why'd you have to come back here, Sloane? You've stirred up nothin' but trouble."

I remained still and calm, contemplating my next move.

"So now what—you're going to shoot me because I know too much?" I said.

"I'm sorry—I didn't want it to happen this way. But you wouldn't let up, and I can't let you get any closer."

"To what?"

The gun shook in his hand like he knew what he had to do but some small fraction of his conscience still resisted.

He hesitated. I swung around, doing a jujitsu crescent kick; it knocked the gun from his hands with the first blow, and sent him spiraling backward with the second.

Jesse scrambled on his hands and knees for the gun, only to find Giovanni's foot resting over it.

Giovanni looked at me. "Get his cuffs."

I removed the cuffs from Jesse's utility belt and tossed them over.

"I thought you'd bust in sooner," I said.

"You're an independent woman, and I knew you could handle yourself." Giovanni looked around. "See if you can find me some rope or tape—either will do."

Giovanni cuffed Jesse's wrists together behind his back and roped him into a kitchen chair. He did it with ease, like a seasoned expert who'd done it many times before.

"You can't do this to me!" Jesse said.

Giovanni smacked Jesse's cheek with the butt of his gun. "Speak when spoken to or I'll gag your mouth as well."

Once Jesse was under control, I reached for the bottle of BUD LIGHT. Jesse grunted and Giovanni gave him a look that kept him quiet. I pulled the bottle off the shelf and it rattled in my hand. I put my eye up to the hole and peered in.

"What is it?" Giovanni said.

I poured out the contents of the bottle and faced them.

"A gold heart-shaped bracelet."

CHAPTER 34

"This belonged to Ivy West," I said, pointing to the bracelet.

Jesse shrugged. "So?"

"She was wearing this the day she disappeared which means you saw her."

"Maybe I did."

"Do you know where she is?"

"Maybe I do."

I glared at him. "You need to tell me."

"What for—it doesn't matter now."

"You were willing to shoot me over it, so I'd say it matters quite a bit."

Jesse smirked. "I don't care what the two of you do to me—I'm not sayin' nothin'."

Giovanni pointed a Ruger .22 at Jesse's foot and fired. The gun made a 'spew' sound that was barely audible thanks to the silencer attached to the end. Jesse howled and shouted a series of expletives, but Giovanni acted like it was nothing and aimed the gun at Jesse's other foot.

"Wait!" Jesse screamed. "Wai...hai...hai...hait! Sloane, do something—help me. How can you stand there and let him do this to me?"

I looked at Giovanni, unsure of what to say. I couldn't believe he actually fired. It may have been the way they solved things in his world, but it wasn't how I did it in mine. Giovanni sensed my frustration and said, "I have no tolerance for men who abuse women and children, Sloane. You're well aware of that."

"But we don't know he did anything to Ivy yet," I said.

"I do."

"How?"

"I'm a good judge of character."

For the second time in a five-minute period, I was speechless. Giovanni took it as a sign to address Jesse himself.

"You have five seconds to tell her about the girl."

Is this really happening?

Giovanni lifted the gun and directed it at Jesse's chest, tilting and re-aiming it for effect with every number he shouted. "Five...four...three..."

"Giovanni, no!" I said.

"Two..."

Jesse squeezed his eyes shut and opened them again. "All right!"

All right?

Jesse looked at me. "Before I say anything—you're way off, Sloane. Ivy couldn't have come back for all of us, so if you're still thinking she's behind this, you're wrong."

"No one knows where she is—how can you be so sure?"

"Because...Ivy's dead. I killed her."

CHAPTER 35

"You killed Ivy!" I said. "Why?"

"She kept calling, asking about Doug, wanting to see me. You don't get it—Ivy couldn't let go."

"Hold on. Back up and start from the beginning," I said. "How did you even know her?"

"We met one night at a party in L.A. Ivy told me where she was from, and I couldn't believe it. I drove to Lancaster and we hung out a couple times. It didn't take long to realize the girl liked to party. And I mean—*hard.* It was more than chugging a few beers—the girl was up for anything."

"So you boys decided, why not take advantage?"

"It just happened. It wasn't like we planned it. We're not animals."

"Who's *we?* All four of you?"

Jesse shook his head.

"It was Nate's idea. He thought it would be fun. Ivy knew, Nate told her."

"You expect me to believe Ivy was up for group sex?"

He nodded.

"We all were—well…the three of us."

"Who wasn't?"

He frowned. "Doug."

"But Alexa is Doug's child, right? He must have changed his mind at some point. What am I missing?"

He sighed but didn't respond. I grabbed his shirt and yanked his body forward. The chair he sat on tipped forward. "Tell me!"

"We, ah…made Doug a rufie-colada."

"A what?"

"Rohypnol," Giovanni said.

"You gave Doug the date rape drug!" I said.

"We thought he needed to loosen up, have some fun," Jesse said. "But then she came back in town a couple months later saying she was pregnant. Doug didn't even realize what that meant at first. The last thing he remembered was kissing her until we told him the truth about what happened."

So how'd she know the baby was Doug's?"

"He was too drugged up to worry about using a condom. None of us thought she'd get pregnant. We were wrong."

"I guess that leaves one question," I said. "Where's Ivy?"

CHAPTER 36

Given the late hour, it was too dark to hike up to the spot he claimed he'd buried Ivy's body after killing her. Giovanni called his men to watch over Jesse so the two of us could go back to the hotel and get some sleep, if that was possible. The string of lies and deception had led me down a path so destructive, even I couldn't believe what was happening. And if what Jesse said was true, and he had killed Ivy, who was responsible for murdering Doug, Rusty, and Nate?

Jesse's version of the night Ivy died started with her coming in town to see him after making a promise to Rosalind never to return again. Jesse turned her away. Rejected, she flew into a rage, clawing and scratching at him with her fingernails. He fought back, striking her in the face, which he alleged he'd only done to calm her down. Ivy was relentless and filled with grief over the loss of her baby. She needed someone to lean on, and had convinced herself the only man for her was Jesse.

Of course, Jesse knew she couldn't stay. Not even if he wanted her to—the risk was too great. There was no way Rosalind would ever allow Ivy to find out the baby was still alive. Jesse felt he needed to protect Doug and the others so he devised a plan. Once Ivy was asleep, he called Doug, Rusty, and Nate and they all came over. Jesse explained their only option was to get rid of her. But how? Jesse's version was Nate suggested murder and talked the others into it. Doug was reluctant, but he too wanted to protect his baby. Now that Ivy was back, there was no telling what she'd do.

At some point during the conversation, Ivy woke and crept to the doorway where she overheard their plans. She tiptoed to the bedroom window and attempted to escape, but Rusty caught her and wrestled her out to the car where her wrists, ankles, and mouth were duct taped and she was tossed into the trunk of the car. They drove to the base of the Tehachapi Mountains, pulled her out of the trunk and set her on the ground while they argued over who would be the one to end her life. When they couldn't reach a decision, Jesse said he'd do the honors, but he needed to be liquored up first. He chugged one beer after the other, tossing the cans on the ground next to Ivy once he was finished. The other men watched in horror, but not one of them did anything to stop him. Once Jesse was past the point of a good buzz, he removed the murder weapon from his jacket pocket: A knife.

The boys carried Ivy until they found a spot they felt was secure, a place no one would ever look for a missing body—but they knew they wouldn't have to worry. No one would know to look there or suspect Ivy's murder was a result of foul play. And so they gathered around. Nate, Doug, and Rusty held her down while Jesse stabbed her over and over again, until she was dead. A shallow grave was dug and her lifeless body was tossed inside.

It didn't matter to me how messed up Ivy West was, she didn't deserve to die. After Jesse spilled his story, I had the urge to stab him myself, but I still needed him. If I was going to find the body, I'd have to rely on him to show me where she was buried. And then I'd make sure her story was told.

***

Back at the hotel, I changed clothes and found Giovanni stretched out on the loveseat reading a newspaper. He folded the paper in half and tossed it on the ground when he saw me enter the room.

"Ready for bed?" he said.

I walked over to the loveseat and sat down. "I need to ask you something."

"I know."

"You do?"

Giovanni stared into my eyes. "You want to know if I would have killed him."

I nodded.

"Not in front of you."

"What if I hadn't been there?" I said.

"But you were, so it wasn't necessary to make a decision."

I wanted to say 'do you do that—you know, kill people,' but I was afraid of the answer. Several months earlier after we'd first met, I searched his name on the internet. It turned out Giovanni had been federally investigated, and not just once, but he was never tried and convicted of any criminal activity. Not yet, anyway. I wondered what it said about me for allowing myself to get involved with someone like him. I was the poster child for individual rights, and yet, Giovanni's crew was at my disposal whenever I was in danger. I knew it, and so did they. How could I stand for justice while accepting their assistance?

"You've gone quiet, luce mia," Giovanni said.

"Just thinking."

He leaned forward and rubbed my hands in his. "I know you wonder about me and what I do, but I need you to understand something—I have never harmed any women or children."

He hadn't, but what about the others?

"Now I want to ask you something," he said. "What will

you do about Jesse when you get the proof you need?"

I leaned back and closed my eyes knowing all I had to do was say the word, and Jesse would never been seen again. "I honestly don't know."

CHAPTER 37

Morning brought a trip to the hardware store for an assortment of shovels. I was surprised when I saw Jesse and noticed someone had taken the time to bandage his foot. Maybe organized crime had a soft spot after all. I didn't. Not for Jesse. I wanted to tear off the bandage and slam my foot on top of his until the pain was like nothing he'd ever felt before. But I needed to be patient. By the end of the day I'd planned to turn him over to the police, and that was enough for me.

The six of us piled into an SUV and followed Jesse's directions. Aside from telling Lucio when to take a left or a right, Jesse stayed quiet. But after what he'd told me the night before, I couldn't.

"I never thought you were capable of such cruelty," I said. "It goes to show I'm a poor judge of character sometimes."

Jesse stared out the window acting like he hadn't heard

me. I opened my mouth to continue, but he said, "Stop. We're here."

One by one we exited the SUV until we were all out. Giovanni's men gathered the tools they needed and we set off. Jesse had been outfitted with a pair of crutches, but even then, it felt like we were moving in slow motion.

After a short walk, I said, "I can't keep this up. Can't he point us in the direction of the body?"

"We're close, but she's right—I can't make it," Jesse said.

Giovanni thought it over and looked at his men who were all out of breath and sweaty like they'd just competed in a triathlon.

"I'll stay with Jesse," Giovanni said. "You three go with Sloane."

"How much farther is this thing?" Lucio said.

Giovanni stepped toward him. "Is there a problem?"

Lucio replied, "No boss—no problem."

I looked around. Trees and bushes dotted the landscape for miles. "Tell me what I'm looking for—a tree, a rock or marker of some kind…"

"A tree," Jesse said. He flattened his hand, turned it to the side, and used it to point us in the right direction. "Follow this straight up. You're gonna walk for about five minutes. You'll come to a wicked-looking tree with blackened branches like it's been burned in a fire. There's an X carved into the base.

You'll wanna dig in front of that X."

It seemed absurd. If I buried someone outdoors, I'd pick the plainest tree I could find so it wouldn't draw attention. Not the one that stood out like a rabbit at a chicken fight.

"How far down is she—five feet or so?" I said.

Jesse shrugged. "More like three."

"Three?"

"We knew nobody was ever gonna find her," Jesse said. "It was late and we were tired."

I gathered the men and we set off. The wind whistled through the trees whipping dust and fragments of weeds into the air. It was strange—eerie. Almost like Ivy knew I was coming to set her free. Several minutes went by and I caught a glimpse of blackened wood. "I think I see it!" I said.

The tree was twisty and viney and looked like it grew right out of a Tim Burton movie. It had to be the one. The men gathered around while I searched the base for an X. It didn't take long for me to find it.

"Right here," I said. "Dig in front of this."

The excavation began, and since I had the power of three, it wasn't long before Lucio shouted, "I feel something!"

The men scraped at the dirt with their hands. I watched, my body stiff, unable to move. I couldn't believe we were actually excavating a hidden grave. Lucio punched his hand down into the soft dirt and then twisted it, trying to grab hold of what he felt before. Seconds later he shouted, "Got it!"

He retracted his hand until it was all the way out and we all gathered around. Everyone had a look of confusion in their eyes. I turned to Lucio. "Keep digging."

CHAPTER 38

"Well," Jesse said. "What did you find?"

I grabbed an object from my pocket and hurled the object in Jesse's direction. It landed at his feet.

He reached down and picked it up with a quizzical look on his face. "You shouldn't have. What's this supposed to be anyway?"

"A message."

"In a bottle?"

He turned it around in his hand.

"Look inside," I said.

Jesse stuck his pinky finger in and pulled out a dirty piece of paper.

"Read it," I said. "Out loud."

JESSE

I SAVED THE BEST FOR LAST

"What is this—some kind of joke?" Jesse said. "Where'd you get this thing?"

"That *thing* was found in the hole where you said Ivy was buried."

"So you found her—her body, I mean?"

I shook my head. "She wasn't there."

He shuddered, terrified. "No…no…no…she has to be. Maybe you weren't in the right spot."

I whipped out my phone and showed him the picture I'd taken of the carving on the tree. "Is this it?"

He nodded.

"The guys dug even deeper than you said—still nothing."

Jesse flung the bottle to the ground. "How's that possible?"

"Obviously she wasn't dead when you guys put her in there."

"But we covered her up—a person couldn't survive that, could they? Even if she wasn't dead, she would have suffocated."

Giovanni gave Jesse a look like he was a total amateur.

"How long did you wait there after she was buried?" I said.

"I dunno. Half hour, maybe less. We wanted to get the hell out of there. It gave us the creeps."

"What's the significance of the BUD LIGHT?" I said.

He shrugged.

"Oh, come on, Jesse. There has to be one. The bottle at your house, the one here. You were drinking it the night you buried Ivy, weren't you?"

Jesse frowned.

One of the men looked at Giovanni. "What you want us to do with him, Boss?"

Jesse's eyes were as wide as saucers. "You've got no proof I did anything to Ivy. Let me go!"

I smiled and retrieved a digital recorder from my pocket. I wiggled it back and forth in front of Jesse. He frowned, well aware of the implications.

"Insurance," I said. "Attempted murder. And you're a cop, so you know how it goes."

Giovanni instructed his men to squeeze Jesse in between them in the back seat until I decided what I wanted to do next.

"Well," I said looking at Giovanni, "I'd say we have our motive. Revenge."

CHAPTER 39

"My baby!" Trista screamed into the phone. "She's missing!"

"For how long?" I said.

"I don't know!"

"Have you called the police?"

"They're on their way—so's Rosalind."

I looked at Giovanni and he turned the car around. I grabbed a piece of paper from the glove box, scribbled Trista's address on it and handed it to him.

"Trista—I need you to take a deep breath and tell me everything that's happened since Alexa left you. Don't leave anything out."

"I don't know if I can, Sloane. I feel like I'm going to pass out—I keep blacking out and grabbing the counter for support."

In that moment, I was glad her twins were at school. They didn't need to see their mom like this.

"If you want me to find her, you have to tell me whatever you can," I said. "I know it's hard. Everything will make sense when I get there, but right now, I need you to keep talking to me."

"Alexa left here Sunday night. She wanted to get back because she had a shift at the hospital the next morning. But she never showed up for it."

"What time did she leave?" I said.

"Around six pm last night."

"Is that the last time you heard from her?"

"Ummm, no. She called me to say she forgot to take the money I left on her nightstand and asked me to mail it out today."

"What time was that?"

"Hold on a sec…"

She pressed a few buttons on her phone. "It was at 6:52 pm."

"Okay, so that explains why she wouldn't have turned around—she'd been driving for almost an hour. Is that all she said?"

"We talked for a minute and she said she was stopping at a gas station."

"Do you know which one?"

"Andy's. She liked to go there because of his custom-made sandwiches."

"What was she driving?" I said.

"2011 Jeep Liberty—Rosalind bought it for her."

"Color?"

"Red."

I relayed the information to Giovanni and he made a call.

"Trista, how did you find out Alexa was missing?"

"She didn't answer any of my phone calls last night. I assumed she was sleeping. We usually talk on her way to work, but when she didn't call to check in, I called the hospital and they said she hadn't shown up. So then I called Alexa's roommate. She said Alexa never came home last night. She assumed she stayed here another day and...."

The line went quiet, but the phone was still engaged. I heard a thud like a hundred pound bag of sugar hitting the floor.

"Trista! Are you still there?"

I turned to Giovanni. "Hurry!"

CHAPTER 40

Andy, of Andy's Gas and Grub, confirmed a red Jeep Liberty had been parked in the corner stall for about eighteen hours. He'd checked his security cameras and saw Alexa exit the car, but she never entered the store. At one point she looked over and walked to the other side of the building like she was meeting someone, but it was beyond the parameters of his security cameras. He'd called police to report the abandoned car, but so far no one had arrived to check it out.

We arrived at Trista's and I sprung from my seat before the car screeched to a stop. A police car pulled up behind us and an officer shouted, "Wait!" But I had no intention of following his orders. Inside the house, Trista was face down on the kitchen floor, drool dripping from the side of her mouth. I stuck two fingers on her neck—she had a pulse.

Her eyes flashed open and she grabbed me. "What happened?"

One of the police officers grabbed me from behind and

attempted to pull me back, but I didn't budge.

"Remove your hands from her," Giovanni said.

The officer spun around and glared at him. "What'd you just say?"

"He said remove…your…hands…from…the…lady. Now," Lucio said.

The officer, who had the thickest mustache I'd ever seen, opened up his mouth to speak but Trista yelled, "Stop! Sloane's here to help find my daughter, and if you want to waste time harassing her, you can leave."

A second officer entered the room. "You can't kick us out of your house ma'am. This is a formal investigation. We have a warrant."

"Show it to me," Giovanni said.

The officers looked at each other and then at Trista like no one had ever called their bluff before. Officer Mustache said, "What can we do to help, ma'am?"

I grabbed Trista's arm and helped her off the ground. There were too many cooks in the kitchen, so I moved her to the sofa while Giovanni got her a glass of water. Once Trista was settled she gave the cops the same information she offered me. I excused myself, leaving Giovanni to look after her best interests, and went into the bedroom where I placed a call to the hospital Alexa worked at.

"Guardian Children's Hospital," a female voice said.

"Hi," I said. "My daughter never showed up for her shift today—Alexa Ward. Could I talk to her supervisor?"

"Hold, please."

In a hushed voice, the woman on the other line spoke to herself as if she was searching some kind of list. Then she returned to the line.

"Her supervisor isn't here right now."

"When will she be back?" I said.

"Says here she's taken a leave of absence."

"For how long?"

The woman sighed into the phone. "I'm not her keeper—I don't know these things."

She went to click the phone down and I said, "Wait! Is there anyone else I could talk to?"

Another deep sigh and then, "Hold on."

I started to say 'thank you' but was cut off when the instrumental version of "You Light Up My Life" streamed through the phone. I considered hanging up, figuring the woman who answered wasn't trying to light up my life, she was trying to ruin it, until a male voice answered.

"This is Doctor Ashby."

"I'm trying to get in touch with Alexa Ward's supervisor," I said.

"And you are?"

"Alexa's mother."

"Funny."

"What?" I said.

"I've met Alexa's mother. Her voice is higher pitched than yours. Should I hang up now?"

I sighed. "I'm a private investigator, who went to school with Alexa's father, and I am in town trying to find clues about what happened to him, but now we have an additional problem: Alexa's missing."

"Why should I believe you?"

"The *real* Trista Ward is in the next room talking to the police," I said. "I can put her on the line."

"Shayna Robbins isn't here right now."

"Who?" I said.

"That's who you'd want to speak with…she's Alexa's supervisor. I'm only in charge of Alexa and a couple other interns during Shayna's absence."

"How long has Shayna been off work?"

"Three weeks, and if you ask me, I hope she stays gone."

"Why?"

"Ever since the new interns started, she hasn't been herself. Especially with Alexa."

"How was she different?" I said.

"Shayna followed Alexa around and tried to get together with her outside of work, and we don't condone relationships between supervisors and staff."

"Can I send you a photo?" I said.

"What for?"

"I'd like you to take a look at it and tell me if you recognize the woman in the photo. Don't pay attention to the hair or the clothes—just the face."

"I guess."

"Great, I'm sending it over now. I'll write my number on the fax."

CHAPTER 41

When I returned to the living room, Officer Mustache was conferring with Officer No-Mustache in the corner. Their whispered banter was interrupted by Rosalind who flew through the door like The Wicked Witch of the West, except she'd forgotten her broom.

"You won't find my granddaughter by standing around," she spat.

Officer Mustache said, "We're following up on some leads now, Mrs. Ward."

"Such as?"

Officer Mustache thumbed in Giovanni's direction. "He just informed us Alexa's car was spotted about an hour from here."

"I don't care about the car—where's my granddaughter!"

Both officers stood there unsure of what to say.

My cell phone vibrated in my pocket and I excused myself from the room. "Thanks for returning my call so quickly," I said.

"I got your fax—and you're right—this is a really old photo, but the face is remarkable. It's like Shayna hasn't aged one bit."

"You're sure the woman in the photo is Shayna Robbins?"

"One hundred percent. But I don't understand. The fax you sent said the woman in the photo is named Ivy West and has been missing for two decades."

"I'm sorry. I wish I could tell you more, but I have to go."

I ended the call and found Trista. "Can I talk to you—alone?"

We entered her bedroom and I locked the door behind me.

"What's going on—do you know something?" Trista said.

I hated this part. "Yes."

Trista grabbed my shoulders and squeezed. "What is it? Tell me!"

"I know where Alexa is—well, not where she is, but who took her. But it won't make sense to you until I tell you everything."

She crossed her arms. "I'm listening."

"This is going to be difficult for you to take—maybe even harder than what you're already going through, but I need you to hear me out."

"What could be worse than a dead husband and a

missing daughter? Who hates me enough to take them both away?"

"It's not about you," I said.

Trista gave me a puzzled look but didn't have the chance to respond before a consistent banging vibrated through the walls.

"Open this door!"

It was Rosalind.

I looked at Trista and indicated with my hand for her to remain seated. "Give me a minute."

I opened the door a crack and peeked out. A disheveled Rosalind was on the other side with her hands on her hips. Her hair was loose and not tightly wound, like it usually was. I'd never seen her so disheveled before.

"Let me in, Sloane," Rosalind said. "What are you two talking about in there?"

"I need some time with Trista. We'll be out in a few minutes."

"You'll come out *now.*"

"Fine, then I'll be talking to the police. About everything."

Rosalind glared at me through the slit in the door like she was trying to figure out if I was bluffing. But I never bluffed, and somewhere inside her manipulative heart, she knew it was time to let go. I'd reached my breaking point. No more secrets. No more lies. Rosalind gave me a you-better-keep-your-mouth-shut look to which I tilted my head to the side, smiled and shut the door—again.

I sat on an armchair across from Trista. "Remember when we talked about the night Alexa was born, and you said Alexa's mother hadn't wanted her?"

She nodded.

"Alexa's birth mother did want her. She was told the baby had died."

"What do you mean?"

"The woman who gave birth to Alexa never wanted to give her up—she wanted to keep her."

"No...that can't be true. Who would do such a..."

And then it came to her.

"Rosalind!"

I nodded.

"Why?"

"Rosalind felt the baby deserved a better life."

"But she can't just..."

"She did."

I pulled a worn paper out of my pocket, unfolded it and handed it to Trista. She scanned it for a moment and then looked at me. "Why does this say she's missing?"

"After Ivy had the baby, she left, but soon after she returned, showing up on Jesse's doorstep and confessing her love for him. He was paranoid she'd find out the truth about the baby among other things, so he called Doug, Nate, and Rusty over."

"I don't understand," Trista said. "Why get all of them involved?"

"The night Ivy got pregnant, she didn't just sleep with Doug."

Trista gasped. "You're saying…it was all of them?"

I nodded.

"Rosalind paid Ivy to leave town and never return again. I'm sure the guys felt confident no one would ever find out about that night, or Alexa. But then Ivy came back, breaking the agreement."

Trista bent her head to the side. "Wait—what are you saying they did?"

"They killed her—or at least they thought they did."

I explained the details of that night to a shaking, wide-eyed Trista. When I finished, she said, "I thought I knew Doug, I really did. But now…"

I leaned over and grabbed her hand. "Doug was drugged the night he slept with Ivy. What happened between them wasn't his fault. But…he did nothing to stop Jesse from ending Ivy's life, and I imagine that haunted him for years. He hated himself for what he'd done."

"Do you think Ivy has my daughter?" She shook her

head. "I feel like I can't even call her that anymore. She had a mother who wanted her, and all this time I thought it was me who was doing her a favor."

"When Alexa started at Guardian Hospital, she was placed under the supervision of a woman named Shayna Robbins."

Trista shrugged. "Why is that important?"

"Because Shayna Robbins is Ivy West."

CHAPTER 42

"So that's how Ivy found out about Alexa—they worked together?"

I nodded.

"I imagine Ivy saw the resemblance right away, but never thought she was her deceased daughter. Alexa must have told Ivy who her parents were at some point, and from there, it wouldn't have been hard for Ivy to put it all together."

Trista stood, her eyes filled with rage. She flew out the bedroom door, scanning the living room for Rosalind. The honesty bus had just swept through town and Rosalind was about to get thrown under it. Trista addressed Officer Mustache. "We need to talk—now."

Rosalind threw herself in front of Trista, blocking her from moving forward. "Let me talk to you first honey, please."

"Save your honey crap for someone else," Trista said. Like Gorbachev's wall, Rosalind remained steadfast, unrelenting. Giovanni glanced at me, and I shook my head. Trista needed this moment, and I wouldn't take it away from her. Her pent up rage released itself in the form of her hands which she thrust into Rosalind's chest, causing Rosalind to go down like a two by four that hadn't been nailed into place. The wall had crumbled.

Trista bent over a frail, shocked woman and no longer felt any fear or respect. "I want you out of my house."

***

While Trista relayed the information I gave her about Rosalind to Officer Mustache and Officer No-Mustache, my phone rang. The caller ID said UNKNOWN.

"Hello?" I said.

"You never quit, do you?"

I motioned to Giovanni to follow me and slipped out the front door.

"Ivy?" I said.

"I wonder…what will you do with Jesse?"

"I could ask you the same thing."

"You've made it impossible for me to get to him, keeping him under house arrest with your little goon squad. I should have started with him first." She laughed. "I saw him climb all over you in the car that night. Shocking, isn't it? How'd it feel to find out he wasn't the man you thought he was all these years?"

"Everything I've found out since arriving here has been disturbing."

"So you know?"

"All of it," I said. "And I'm sorry for what you've been through."

"I don't need your sympathy!" she snapped. "When was the last time you were stabbed and left for dead?"

I backed off. The last thing I wanted was for her to hang up.

"Jesse didn't believe me when I told him you weren't where he buried you."

"Of course he didn't. They were all too drunk to realize I was still breathing. I stayed still, not even flinching when he tossed me into that hole, breaking my wrist. They didn't even stay five minutes after they covered me with dirt. Their stupidity saved my life."

"Why not turn them in?" I said.

"I knew Rosalind would hire them the best lawyer money could buy and I'd end up in some psych ward with a bunch of crazies. It was easier to change my name, disappear, and never return again. And I had the money to do it, so I took off and started a new life."

"But then you met Alexa."

"The first time I looked into her eyes, I knew she was mine. I just knew it. When I asked her where she was from and who her parents were, I didn't want to believe it was true. My baby was alive and all grown up right in front of me."

"You should know Trista is innocent in all this," I said. "Rosalind told her you gave the baby up. Trista gave her a great life."

"And robbed me of mine!"

"She would have given her back to you—no matter how much it would have pained her. Trista never would have kept Alexa from her birth mother."

"It doesn't matter now. Alexa's a grown woman. All the memories I could have had of her childhood, gone. How could she ever think of me as her mother now? When she finds out I killed her father, she'll hate me."

"Have you told her who you are—does she know why you took her?"

The line went silent.

"Ivy? Are you there?" I said.

"Mom?"

"Alexa," I said. "Is that you?"

I turned to Giovanni. "See if you can get Trista out of the house discreetly."

He nodded and went inside.

"Alexa, this is Sloane. I'm trying to get your mom for

you. Are you okay?"

"Yeah, but I'm scared."

"Can you tell me where you are or where you're going?"

Silence.

"Okay," I said, "I know Ivy is standing right next to you. Can you give me a hint?"

"Who's Ivy?" Alexa said.

"You know her as Shayna."

"Tell my brothers I'll be home soon, and we can play Ben 10."

Trista rushed through the door and seized the phone from my hands. "Alexa, honey. Are you okay? Mommy's here. Tell me how to find you."

"Put it on speaker," I whispered.

In the background Ivy said, "Tell her...tell her what I said!"

"Shayna says she's my mom," Alexa whispered. "She said you took me from her when I was a baby. Why is she saying that?"

Trista looked at me, a look of paranoia on her face.

"Tell her not to do anything to make Shayna upset. You'll explain everything later."

Once that was relayed, Ivy grabbed the phone. "You've had Alexa her entire life. It's my turn!"

Tears streamed down Trista's face. "I didn't know—

Sloane told me everything about an hour ago. Please don't hold your anger against Alexa. She's scared. I'll do anything to work this out—whatever you want."

The phone clicked, and the line went dead.

CHAPTER 43

"I'll need your phone," Officer Mustache said to me. Meanwhile Officer No-Mustache was going over what had just transpired with the chief of police who'd arrived a few minutes earlier. Rosalind had been detained in the back of a police car and looked like she couldn't believe they were serious about arresting her.

"Your phone?" he said—again.

"Not yet," I said.

"I wasn't asking."

"I understand, and you'll have it, after Ivy calls back."

"What makes you think she will?"

"Ivy's past has hardened her," I said, "but I'd like to believe she won't take it out on Alexa."

"Your hunch isn't enough."

Giovanni intercepted our conversation long enough for me to walk away, phone in hand.

Behind me, the police chief addressed Officer No-

Mustache. "You haven't heard from Jesse today, have you?"

He shook his head. "Why?"

The chief continued. "He took the day off, but we need him. Can't get him to answer his phone though."

Officer No-Mustache said, "You want me to check his house?"

"I need you here," the chief said. "But do me a favor, call him every once in a while and see if you can get him to answer. I need to make some calls, get the big guns out here to help find our missing girl."

My phone vibrated, but this time, I couldn't hide it. All eyes were on me when I answered until the phone was snatched from my hands by Officer Mustache.

"This is Officer Stevens. Is this Ivy West?"

Giovanni gave him a look that indicated he would pay for his mistake, but Ivy was already making him pay, with her silence.

"Ms. West, are you there?" Officer Stevens said.

Thankfully, he had her on speaker. The chief put his finger to his lips like we were school children, unaware of the need to keep quiet.

"Put Sloane on the phone," Ivy said.

"Can't do that. She's not a family member or a part of law enforcement—we'll be taking over from here. Why don't you talk to me—tell me what it will take to get Alexa home safe?"

"Put Sloane on or you won't hear from me again."

"Wait!"

"What?"

"Tell me what you want," Officer Stevens said. "What can we do to resolve this situation?"

She laughed. "This *situation*? I want the last twenty years of my life back. I want my baby. I want the night I was raped to have never happened. And most of all, I want Officer Jesse Tucker to suffer the way I suffered. Can you do that for me—can you make it all go away?"

He went silent, looking at the chief for what to say next.

Ivy laughed. "I didn't think so."

She ended the call, and the chief looked over at his officers, clueless about why Jesse had been brought up in the conversation. A few minutes later, Trista tugged on my sleeve and slanted her head toward the guest bathroom. We walked inside. She pressed a finger to my lips and held the screen of her cell phone in front of me. A text message said:

SHOW THIS TO SLOANE IF YOU WANT TO SEE ALEXA
AGAIN.
I AM WILLING TO MAKE A TRADE: JESSE FOR ALEXA.
ONE HOUR. TELL NO ONE.
I'LL BE IN TOUCH.

CHAPTER 44

I needed quiet, a place where I could go and think, free from the noise and chaos around me. But when I walked outside, I couldn't take my eyes off Rosalind and her pathetic realization that she was being whisked away in the back of a squad car where any passerby could see.

I walked up and tapped the window, but she refused to look at me.

"The truth needs to come out," I said. "And if it doesn't, I'll come in to make sure they know the facts. And I mean *all* the facts."

Without moving her head, the window came down. "That piece of white trash won't last one day after I find her. And as for you, Sloane, I'll ruin your life just like you tried to ruin mine."

"Take a look at yourself and realize who really tore apart your family," I said. "It sure as hell wasn't me."

I retreated to the SUV, closed the door, and locked

myself in. The thought of handing Jesse over was somewhat appealing considering who he turned out to be. It certainly seemed like a fair trade—one innocent girl for an attempted murderer and rapist. All his talk about how Ivy was 'up for it' the night of the party—lies. Of course, I never believed it. Not after the moves he made on me in his car.

But it wasn't the reason I'd retreated to the solitude a warm vehicle had to offer. I did my best thinking in silence. I closed my eyes, removed all the words from Ivy's conversations and concentrated on one thing. The background. During her first phone call, I heard the duh-dum of wheels passing over bumpy patches of pavement in the road. Ivy was driving—but where?

What else did I hear? The chugging of a train as it passed through town. Tehachapi was known for its single-track railway; it was one of the busiest in the world. By now Ivy knew people we looking for her. She needed to hide, but where could she go? There wasn't anyone for her to turn to—but she was headed somewhere.

I concentrated on the second call. Again, the sound of a train, but when she talked I noticed something—her voice wasn't clear. There was an echo, like she was talking inside of something. A building? No. A car? No. A tunnel?

Yes!

I opened the door and tried to conceal my joy as I

approached Giovanni. I hoisted myself onto my tiptoes and whispered into his ear. "I know where she is."

***

"You can't do this!" Jesse squealed.

"I can—and it's what you deserve," I said.

"You're okay handing me over without leaving me a way to defend myself?"

"What about Ivy? Who was around to defend her? No one."

"Can you at least tell me where we're going?"

Lucio jerked his elbow to the side, smashing Jesse in the gut. "Enough out of you. No more talkin', ya hear me?"

"When I was on the phone with Alexa," I said, "she mentioned playing a game with her brothers, Ben 10. Well, the game does exist, and there's actually more than one. Thing is, Trista's son's don't own it."

"What's that supposed to mean?" Lucio said.

"When Alexa mentioned the name of the game, I had just asked her if she could give me a hint about where she was at or where Ivy was going."

"I still don't get it," Lucio said.

Giovanni looked like he wanted to give his own guy the elbow.

"During the call I heard noises in the background," I said. "The road, the train, and then an echoing sound. She's in the number ten tunnel."

My phone rang.

"Ivy?"

"Do you have Jesse?"

"I do," I said.

"Before I give you my location, I want proof."

I held the phone up to Jesse. "Say something."

He shook his head.

I put my 9mm to the center of his forehead. "Speak!"

"You won't shoot—you need me," Jesse said.

I smiled and brought the phone back up to my ear. "Satisfied?"

"Same Jesse…smug as ever."

"Tell me where to meet," I said.

"You're alone, right? Just you and Jesse?"

"I haven't said a word to the cops if that's what you're worried about. Now…where are you?"

Ivy gave me the location, said to be there in one hour.

Lucio shrugged. "Why an hour?"

"She's waiting," I said. "It isn't time yet."

"For what?"

"The train."

CHAPTER 45

The railway line that ran from Bakersfield through Tehachapi and out past Mojave was built in 1874 by the Southern Pacific Railroad. Thousands of Chinese workers were brought in to cut through solid and decomposed granite. They used everything from pick axes to blasting powder, and in less than two years, the job was complete. Many tunnels were carved into the mountains, allowing trains to pass through, but not all of them stood the test of time.

Tunnel ten wasn't far from the Tehachapi Loop. It was named the Loop because of the circular rotation the train took when it passed over and under itself. Even after one hundred years of wear and tear on the rails, more than thirty trains still passed through on any given day.

We parked as close as we could get to the tunnel before hiking over to it. As soon as I exited the SUV, I flashed back to memories of seeing the train as a child. In my mind, when the train sounded its horn before it entered the tunnel it was saying goodbye, because once it entered, it disappeared, like the mountain had opened its mouth and swallowed it whole. But then, like magic, seconds later the train would re-emerge as it pushed through the opening on the other side.

It had been twenty minutes, and not the hour Ivy wanted, but there was something to be said for the element of surprise. An abandoned Lexus was parked nearby. The doors were locked, but when I peered through the window I saw a headband on the passenger seat. It was black with a white flower and tiny black feathers shooting off the side of it. Alexa wore it the first night we met.

"Alexa's here," I said to Giovanni. "At least, I hope she is…"

We left Giovanni's men in the SUV with the idea that less was more in this situation and walked in the direction of the tunnel with Jesse. Giovanni made it clear Jesse wasn't to utter one word, and so far, he was complying. Once we got through the weeds and the patchy terrain, I spotted the mouth of the tunnel. It was just like I remembered. A grey concrete-like substance shaped into an oval archway that seemed just wide enough for the train to pass through.

One of my hands clutched Jesse's arm like a claw in a stuffed animal machine at the supermarket and the other hovered over my gun.

"Stop," I said. "I want to listen."

But it was still. Even the air. Neither voices nor movement echoed through the tunnel. It was as if the structure itself had been left for dead.

I looked at Giovanni. "How much time?"

"We're still thirty minutes out."

"Good." I turned to Jesse who was limping at such a slow pace we practically pulled him along. "Keep walking, and if you want to come out of this alive, don't do anything to screw this up, or I *will* hand you over."

Both Jesse and Giovanni's eyes widened.

"You're not making the trade—you'd do that for me?" Jesse said.

From the stony look on Giovanni's face, he wondered the same thing. Second chances weren't part of the mafia handbook. There were no three-strikes-and-you're-out options; one strike was more than enough to send any man to the grave, and the grimace on Giovanni's face told me he wanted to do just that. But dying wasn't the only way Jesse could pay for his crimes, and prison suited me just fine.

I was confident about putting Jesse away for life, but when it came to Ivy, my thoughts were hazy—a grey cloud had formed in my mind I never knew existed. For the first time, I didn't just see things as black or white. But no matter what she'd been put through, one thing was clear: Ivy was still a murderer.

I had Jesse and Giovanni stay out of sight while I walked up to the entrance of the tunnel. It was dark. I could see inside, but after several feet the track curved around, leaving a blind spot on the other side. I had to decide—would I walk in and look around the corner, or would I shout her name and wait for a response? I knew the tunnel wasn't long, so there was a good chance once I rounded the corner, Ivy would be waiting there for me.

I glanced at my cell phone. Twenty-five minutes until our scheduled rendezvous. I had time. I took one step forward knowing no matter how light my steps, there was a good chance she'd hear me coming. And she did.

"Who's there?" Ivy said.

I couldn't see her, but I knew she was close.

"It's Sloane."

"You're early—you aren't supposed to be here yet. How'd you get here so fast?"

"Doesn't matter. I want to talk."

"There's nothing more to say. Where is he?"

"Nearby."

"Send him in."

"Send Alexa out," I said.

"No—not yet."

"Alexa," I shouted, "are you in here?"

"Save it—she isn't. And if you want her back, you'll have

to keep up with your end of our agreement."

"I only brought Jesse here to trade," I said. "No Alexa, no exchange."

"Then you can go. We're done here."

I heard footsteps like she was sliding out the tunnel, keeping her back to the wall so she remained out of sight.

"Ivy...wait."

The side-stepping stopped, but she said nothing.

"I know why you kidnapped Alexa," I said. "You never wanted to hurt her—you thought it was the only way you could get your hands on Jesse once we had him. The last loose end you needed to tie up. The one you wanted to hurt the most. But why not bring Rosalind along too? The woman who lied to you, took your child. Why spare her life? And Doctor Robinson's?"

Ivy's cackle echoed through the air.

"The good doctor is dead. And as for Rosalind, that old crow's dead too."

"Impossible," I said. "When I left her she was in the back of a squad car headed for the police station to be booked for her crimes. There's no way you could have killed her."

"I didn't. She killed herself."

"I don't understand," I said.

Stage four cancer. It won't be long now, and I'd rather she suffer knowing I killed her son. Death is the one thing she can't control."

And the revelations kept pouring out.

"Why the tunnels?" I said. "What's the significance of this place?"

"Ask Jesse—he dragged me here."

I pictured a young, innocent girl around eighteen going for a car ride with a group of boys. "We want to show you something," they would have said. And she would have felt the attention she'd been deprived of most of her life. Once they reached the tunnel, Ivy probably swooned over how cool it seemed at night. And then one of the boys walked her in— Jesse perhaps—and, pushing her up against the stony wall, he had his way with her. When her shock turned to tears, he tagged in another, and then another, until she didn't even fight it anymore.

"You don't need to kill Jesse to make him pay for what he's done."

"Yes, I do!" Her voice cracked. "Send him in, now! Then I'll tell you where to find Alexa."

"Why the rush? The train comes in a few minutes. What are you planning?"

"Three minutes, Sloane," was her only reply.

I had to think fast. I didn't believe any harm had come to Alexa, but I was concerned once she had Jesse, Ivy would keep Alexa for herself. Was she using the commotion from the train to plan her getaway?

Giovanni pulled Jesse to the opening of the tunnel. "Send him," he whispered. "Once he's in, I'll go around the other side to make sure she doesn't escape out the back."

"What—wait, no!" Jesse stammered. "You can't."

But I needed to do something.

"I have Jesse," I yelled. "Come out where I can see you, Ivy."

"I want you and the man you're with to throw your guns into the tunnel. And not some sissy throw, either. Hurl them far enough that I can see them."

We did as she instructed, and once she saw them smack down on the rocky floor in front of her, Ivy pushed herself off the wall and appeared on the center of the track. She held her hand out for Jesse.

"I won't go," Jesse said.

"If I don't get Alexa back, I'll kill you myself," I said. "Move—now."

He hesitated and Giovanni shoved him so hard he almost flew to the ground and then he limped forward. In the background, the train chugged along, moving at full speed.

"Stay in the center of the track," Ivy yelled to Jesse.

"But the train is coming—are you insane!" Jesse yelled.

At this point in her life, she probably was.

"Do you remember, Jesse? Do you remember now!"

she shouted. "You didn't need to kill me the night I returned to town—I was already dead…inside."

Two tugs from the conductor sounded the alarm, the train was about to enter the tunnel. I looked at Jesse; he trembled with fear. This had been her plan all along—she meant for him to die here. And I couldn't do it. As much as he deserved what was coming to him, I couldn't stand there and watch it happen.

I raced inside the tunnel. Jesse froze as if waiting for the inevitable to happen, but then I tackled him. We collapsed into shards of rock and I pressed my head into the ground while the train whizzed by. It was the longest three minutes of my life, but finally, the train exited.

Before I could open my eyes, Giovanni had lifted me off the ground and clutched me to him. I tried to turn, to see what had become of Ivy, but Giovanni's hands pressed into my cheeks. "Don't turn around," he said.

"Is she…dead?"

He nodded.

Jesse looked up at the two of us. "A little help, please."

"Help yourself," I said.

"But I thought…?"

"What?" I said. "Because I saved you I developed some sort of soft spot? It was the right thing to do. And now I get to make sure everyone in town knows who you really are. I want you to live the rest of your life knowing your friends died because of you."

Giovanni looked down at me—he couldn't have been more proud. I leaned my head on his shoulder and we walked to the car. I hoped to find clues about Alexa's whereabouts in Ivy's Lexus. Giovanni sent his men back for Jesse, who had made a failed attempt at hobbling away.

"Wait a minute," I said.

Giovanni stopped.

"Do you hear something?"

A sound emanated from the hill beside us—whimpering—like someone was calling out but unable to speak any words.

I ran up the hill and stopped. There, on the other side, was Alexa. She was gagged and tied to a tree. A piece of folded up paper had been taped to the back of her shirt. Giovanni loosened the bandana wadded up inside her mouth and then pulled out a Swiss Army Knife and sliced the rope from her wrists. Once she was free, she threw her arms around me. "I love you, Sloane. I'll love you forever. Thank you. Thank you. Thank you!"

A feeling I rarely experienced crept up my stomach until it created a pit inside my throat and I choked up. This was what my job was all about.

I pulled the note off her back. It was addressed to

Alexa. I handed it to her.

"I don't want this," she said. "You read it and then do me a favor and get rid of it."

I unfolded the letter and read in silence.

Dear Alexa,

I'm sorry about what happened. I never meant to take you, and I never meant for you to get hurt in all this, but I'm sure you have been. Even after I thought you died, I always loved you. I thought of my precious daughter every day. But you grew up not knowing me, and that's a pain I can't live with anymore. I would rather be dead than not be in your life. I've watched Sloane over the past few weeks. She's a good woman, and I believe she'll tell you the truth about what happened. I hope one day you can forgive me for your father and for leaving you now. Death is a fitting end, and I welcome it. You're an amazing woman, and I know you'll be a wonderful mother one day. I'll be watching. Maybe then I can finally become part of your life. - Mom

CHAPTER 46

Giovanni came around the corner and stared into the bedroom. "Ready?"

I nodded. "I feel like I've overstayed my welcome, but I learned something. Once I got away from my dad, I had some good memories here. This town reminded me of all the things I'd forgotten. I had so many bad experiences as a child, I forgot about the good ones."

Giovanni smiled and kissed my forehead. "The plane is fueled and ready, whenever you are."

"I'll just be a minute."

Giovanni clicked the remote and the TV came on, but then he disappeared.

How odd, I thought.

I checked the room for anything I might have left and grabbed the remote to turn off the TV. The local news interrupted *The View* to discuss a blazing fire in Bear Valley Springs. On Black Forest Drive. On the street I grew up on.

In the house I wanted to forget. And I remembered what I'd said to Giovanni in the car that day: *I'd strike a match and burn it to the ground if I could, and then I'd watch until every last piece of it was gone forever.*

I zipped up my bag and smiled. It was time to go home.

***

Stephen King once said:
"MONSTERS ARE REAL, AND GHOSTS ARE REAL TOO.
THEY LIVE INSIDE US. AND SOMETIMES, THEY WIN."

***

For MORE ABOUT Cheryl Bradshaw'S books:

Blog: cherylbradshawbooks.blogspot.com
Website: cherylbradshaw.com
Facebook: CherylBradshawBooks
Twitter: @cherylbradshaw
Pinterest: @cherylbradshaw

Printed in Great Britain
by Amazon